J I GRECO

ROAD TRIPS #1

TAKE THE ALL-MART!

WHOLESALE ATOMICS

ISBN (Paperback): 978-1-964666-05-1
ISBN (E-Book): 978-1-964666-15-0

Published by Wholesale Atomics.

Chapter 1

SUNDAY DRIVE, WITH CANNIBALS

The tricked-out, inch-thick depleted uranium armor-scaled '73 Dodge *Swinger* called the *Festering Wound* hauls ass through the Wasteland down the cracked and cratered, debris-strewn remains of I-80 on adaptiplastic tires, her breeder reactor thrumming dangerously close to red-line.

Behind her wheel, Trip's plugged into the dash and driving with his mind through the coiled patch cord jacked into the socket behind his right ear. The steering wheel jerks freely on its own, Trip's eyebrows twitching to swerve the *Wound* around long-abandoned cars and potentially Dodge-swallowing potholes.

"You know," Trip says, taking a final drag off one hand-rolled cig, jabbing it out in the overflowing dashboard ashtray, and immediately lighting a new one with the car lighter, "I'm seriously thinking about giving up this whole reprobate adventurer thing and going into accounting."

Trip was 23, tall and wiry, pale and twitchy, with jet-black hair sculpted into a Jack Lord curl. He wore a grime-caked long-tailed tux jacket with the collar popped and the sleeves rolled up to the elbow, a t-shirt that simply read "Game Over", ripped, faded black jeans, and red canvas hi-tops kept together with duct tape.

"Have you ever given any thought to lion taming?" Rudy asked, along with the sound of a zipper being yanked down, all wet and mushy.

"No good — I'm allergic to chairs." Trip glanced over at Rudy in the passenger seat, and instantly regretted it. He winced, quickly looked away. "Vishnu's nipples, man, can't you keep your hands out of there for five fuckin' minutes?"

"Not if I want to keep my buzz going, I can't, no. I'm burning through mix like nobody's business today. I blame stress. By which, of course, I mean you." Rudy was 22, compactly stocky but muscular, with ruddy skin and a flame-red soul patch. He was already balding. What hair he had left jutted out in curly tufts from under a crumpled leopard-print fez. He wore a Peace-symbol t-shirt under an ammo bandolier, forest camo parachute pants, and steel-toed hikers.

Rudy plunged a hand through the zippered opening in his own stomach, pushing aside intestines to rummage around in his guts with practiced abandon. "'Let's go East', you said." Rudy's fingers found what he was looking for hiding behind his spleen. "They love us in the Wasteland." A twist and a hiss and he pulled out a thumb-sized cylinder, empty and dripping with viscera. "Ass."

Rudy tossed the empty over his shoulder into the back seat, then slid a fresh, full cartridge out of his bandolier. Biting his lip, he shoved the cart into his gut, squirmed around to fit it into place. A twist the other way and with a sharp hum the chemical synthesis plant in his belly came back online, refueled, almost instantly re-flooding his bloodstream with fresh THC-analog. Rudy went all content and withdrew his hand, zipping his stomach back up and patting his hairy belly. "Ahh, sweet pseudo-cannabis bliss. I'm ready for death, now."

Trip snorted. "We're not gonna die."

"I don't see how that's possible." Rudy wiped the viscera from his hand on his camos and pulled his t-shirt down. "Unless they've all of a sudden given up and gone away?"

Trip glanced into the driver's side-view mirror. The Magnums were still on their ass, the whole mind-linked, cannibalistic howling mad WOLFpack of them, weaving after the *Wound* half-a-meter off the road on plutonium battery-powered sonic surfboards. Two dozen of them, maybe more. Obsessed with the old TV private eye, they all looked like prime 1980's Tom Selleck, even the women, thanks to sloppy amateur elective plastic surgery, cheesy hair-plug mustaches, and tattered Hawaiian shirts. Each one had a whip antenna grafted onto a temple, the tips of the antennas blinking angry red in staccato unison. They brandished a variety of weapons: nail-encrusted baseball bats, crowbars with spikes welded to their tips, sawed-off shotguns, and one severed leg with the foot wrapped in razor wire.

"No, apparently not." Trip took a long draw from his cig. "We're out of grenades, aren't we?"

"Yeah, you used them all back at that sports bar in Albuquerque winning that Karel Capek bobblehead alarm clock from those robo-bikers."

Trip smiled proudly. "Showed them how real men play Candyland."

"You just had to have it, didn't you?"

"It was near-mint-in-box. It's a collector's item."

"Which you promptly threw in the trunk and haven't looked at since." Rudy scratched his soul-patch, thinking, then snapped his fingers. "What about the autocannon? Just flip us around, charge the bastards and open fire."

"You traded the last box of shells for two dozen donuts outside of Indy."

Rudy went sheepish. "Did I?"

"Yeah. In the future, let's just assume we'll need ammo more than food and not trade it away."

"But they had sprinkles."

"Even for sprinkles." Trip twitched his left eyebrow to have the *Wound* avoid the burnt-out husk of a semi cab, then smirked over at Rudy. "You wouldn't want to throw yourself out the window, would you? If you tuck and roll, maybe you'll knock a couple over. Probably won't stop them, but it'll give me a much needed chuckle."

"May I suggest a rail gun?" came a clearly fake English-accented voice from the back seat.

Trip huffed. "Yeah, that'd be nice. Too bad we don't have a rail gun."

"No. But we do."

Trip and Rudy looked at each other in surprise, then back at the Higgins, bound in electrical tape and smiling smugly at them from the back seat. The WOLFpack's hub, he was done up like a proper, prissy English gentlemen about to set off on a jungle adventure, complete with a fraying safari outfit and pith helmet. A pair of extra-long whip antennas grafted onto his temples stick up through holes crudely cut in the helmet's brim.

"You ain't got no railgun," Trip said, then raised an eyebrow at Rudy. "Do they?"

Rudy shrugged. "I didn't see any..." His side-view was long-gone missing in action, so to check he had to poke his head out the window, clamping a hand over his fez to keep it from flying off.

In the rear of the pack, a female Magnum was un-slinging a long, thin-barreled rifle from her back. She tossed it to a short Filipino Magnum bobbing in front of her. He in turn tossed it to the Magnum in front of him, and so on. The rifle worked its way up through the weaving pack, tossed from Magnum to howling Magnum, finally arcing through the air at the back of the burly, toothless Magnum at the head of the pack. At the last possible moment, the leader spun, clutching the rifle out of the air, and continued spinning, leveling and aiming the rifle at the *Wound* as he completed the three-sixty.

Rudy pulled his head back in, his face serenely grave. "Looks like a Norwegian special action stock with a knock-off Israeli straight-bore accelerator." He twist-ed around to ask the Higgins: "What are they using? Tungsten slugs?"

The Higgins smiled at him. "What else?"

Cig dangling from his lips, Trip looked at Rudy. "Think they'll be able to get through the armor —"

He cut himself off as, out of the corner of his eye, he saw the Higgins suddenly jog his head to the side. Trip had just enough time to duck himself before the —

POP!

Where the Higgins' head had been a second before he moved, a half-inch hole had just simply appeared in the armor scaling over the rear window, the edges of the hole glowing white hot. A matching exit hole had appeared almost instantaneously in the windshield, right under the rear-view.

"Vishnu's aunt Patty." Trip stared at the hole in the windshield as he sat up. "That missed me by way too little."

Staring back at the entry hole and past the grinning Higgins, Rudy reached under his t-shirt to give his left nipple a good twist, turning the flow of THC-analog from his belly factory all the way up. "Too late to go to Rehoboth, isn't it?"

Trip gave him a curt smirk, then twisted to sneer back at the Higgins. "Go ahead, be all smug. They could have hit you, you know."

"They know exactly where I am," the Higgins said. "That's how this works. My pack sees, hears, feels, and shares every thought I have."

Rudy balled a fist and punched the Higgins in the eye. "How'd they like sharing that?"

The Higgins shrugged it off, chuckling even as his eye socket began to redden and his eyelid puffed up.

"What's so funny?" Rudy asked, kissing his knuckles and shaking his fingers out.

"I'm telling them to put the next one between your shoulder blades."

Trip took a long suck of his cig, titled his head back to blow smoke at the duct-taped patched ceiling. "Rudy, I'm going to need a moment to think. Alone."

Rudy nodded enthusiastically and grabbed the stun baton off the dash. "Goodnight, you prince of mind-sharing freaks," he said as he twisted around and jammed the baton into the Higgins' neck, triggering it on contact.

The Higgins convulsed with a gurgled yelp, eyes rolling to white before he gave a final shudder and went limp, unconscious. Rudy kept pulsing him until the Higgins slumped over, cheek slapping against the seat cushion, and his antenna tips started erratically blinking yellow, connection with the WOLFpack lost.

Rudy settled back into his seat, tossing the baton up onto the dash. "Not that that didn't feel satisfying on a whole number of levels, but they've still got that railgun."

Trip flicked his cig out the window and reached into his tux jacket to take an ancient Bugs Bunny Pez dispenser from one of the dozen utility pockets sewn into it. He tipped the head back to pop a chalky home-made tablet into his mouth, where it dissolved almost instantly, the mix of 500 mg caffeine, 200 mg evaporated distilled iguana urine, and a spritz of bug spray for extra kick and flavor hitting him like a happily runaway freight train. Nerve endings pleasantly on fire and smirking like a madman, he tucked the plastic rabbit gently away, and closed his eyes to commune with the *Wound*. "They're not gonna fire without his lordship-eyes-and-ears back there telling them where to aim. They won't risk hitting him."

"So that's the plan?" Rudy asked. "Just keep him knocked out while we drive until we hit the Atlantic and drown?"

Trip's eyes darted spastically under closed lids. "Let's call that Plan B for now."

"Is there a Plan A?"

Trip's eyes snapped opened. "Grab something."

Without giving Rudy a chance to actually grab something, Trip sent the *Wound* swerving hard off the old interstate, plunging down an embankment and into what, a century ago, had been fertile farmland but was now nothing but rocky, withered scrubland. With a twitch of his eyebrow the *Wound*'s adaptaplastic tires tightened for off-road and her suspension bucked, the car rising up six inches for better ground clearance as it bumped and jostled over the rough ground.

Rudy popped his head out the window for a quick look behind them. "In case you're wondering, nope, they didn't fall for it. And look at that — they can move faster and better on those boards of theirs out here than we can. How could we have possibly guessed that? They're going to catch us. And eat us. Thanks."

Trip smirked back at him. "For someone with a THC plant in their belly you worry a hell of a lot." He snapped his fingers at the *Wound*'s brain, a salvaged, rebuilt, and heavily augmented Sega GameGear, wedged tight into a crude cutout in the center of the dash above the stock AM radio. The game system's two-inch screen snapped on to show a very low-resolution version of the high-bandwidth, immersive sensor telemetry the *Wound* was feeding Trip through the patch cord mind-machine link. "MODAR's picked up something a couple miles past this hill. If it's what I think it is, it could just be our Plan A."

Rudy squinted at the tiny, 32-color screen. A blip representing the *Wound* headed full-tilt towards a solid line. "What, a cliff we can *Thelma and Louise* off of?"

"You wish." Trip jogged his chin to point out the windshield just as the *Wound* crested the hill. "Hell... I wish."

Rudy looked out. Took a few seconds for his eyes to go wide and his jaw slack. "That's not? It can't be..."

"It is," Trip said, swallowing.

A couple miles ahead a jagged, broiling wall of smoke and dust stretched across the valley from mountain to mountain, thirty feet high. Behind that, for something like a couple hundred miles back, was a rooftop pocked with thousands of HVAC units and triangular solar collectors, panels glinting red in the dawn sun.

Trip nudged Rudy with an elbow. "Wake him up."

Rudy reluctantly tore his attention away and grabbed the stun baton, twisting and reaching into the back seat to poke its non-electric handle end into the Higgins side until the man grunted.

"We're off-road?" The Higgins stirred, his antenna tips blinking steady red again as he re-established contact with his WOLFpack. "How thoughtful of you. I was afraid we wouldn't be able to catch up to you on open road..." His voice trailed off as he sat up and saw through the windshield what the *Wound* was speeding towards, and when he spoke again, it was practically a whisper. "By Robin Masters... it's an All-Mart."

"Yup," Rudy said. "And us heading straight for it. Imagine that?"

The Higgins' voice — and accent — cracked. "You wouldn't?"

Trip gave the Higgins a sharp, devilish smirk through the rear-view. "Drive straight into it? What a great idea."

"No, you can't!" the Higgins yelled, his real accent — a Southern drawl, from around Shreveport — coming through loud and clear. "You know what that is? What happens in there?"

Trip took out a fresh cig and lit it. "Midnight showings of *Rocky Horror* and *Darkstar*?"

"People get turned into zombies!" the Higgins yelled. "Anybody that goes in!"

"The living, shopping nano-dead," Rudy said with a chuckle. "Or so I hear."

"Well," Trip said, "that sounds like something I'd like to see." He twisted around to point the cig at the Higgins. "Of course, your guys will have to follow us in, right? They can't get too far away from their hub, and even if you commanded them not to, they'd have to come after you, right into the heart of zombie central. It's the downer flip-side of the WOLFpack tech. They'll be compelled to follow you to their deaths. Tragic, really. No wonder the military dumped the tech." Trip shrugged at Rudy. "Well, what ya gonna do?"

"Stop!" the Higgins shrieked, throwing his body around the backseat in absolute panic. "Turn around!"

"Why?" Trip asked. "Just so you can... why are you chasing us, anyway?"

Realizing he was boxed in, the Higgins gave up throwing his body around and sat back, sweating and panting. "There's a considerable bounty."

Trip raised an eyebrow at him. "Bounty?"

"Courtesy of the Warlord Hu."

Rudy glared accusingly at Trip. "She put a bounty on us?"

Trip shot him an unapologetic smirk, then asked the Higgins: "The little minx put a bounty on us?"

The Higgins's practiced, affected calm returned and he primly smiled at Trip. "The bounty's on you. Him," he said, his English accent back, nodding his head at Rudy, "she didn't mention, so we planned on making a nice summer sausage for the mid-solstice feast."

"Can't this thing go any faster?" Rudy asked, turning to glare out the windshield, crossing his arms over his chest.

The broiling wall of the All-Mart's expansion front was already less than a mile away, slowly and inexorably swallowing and converting everything in its path into raw materials for the massive structure's slow expansion down the valley, a meter a day.

Trip twitched an eyebrow and the *Wound* sped up. The Higgins let out a whimper.

"For the record, Rudy, I apologize for nothing," Trip said, taking a long drag off his cig.

Rudy growled. "You know you're the first person I'm eating after I go zombie, right?"

"I'd be offended if I weren't," Trip said. "I hear my inner thighs are particularly tasty. They'd probably go best with a balsamic and red wine reduction."

"What doesn't?" Rudy said, tweaking his nipple through his t-shirt for as much THC-analog as his stomach factory would give him.

Trip nodded, blew smoke at the windshield. "True."

They were close enough now that they could see the tendrils within the All-Mart's broiling expansion front. Thick, billowing and serpentine, they flicked out, grabbing rocks, shrubs, anything within reach, drawing it all back into the All-Mart for breakdown and repurposing.

"If you've got any last words for your WOLFpack," Trip said to the Higgins, "I'd think them now."

"Wait!" the Higgins yelled. "What if we forgot we ever caught up with you?"

Trip twitched. Brakes engaged instantly, sending the *Wound* into a controlled fishtail on the loose scrubland dirt. When she finally stopped swinging around, her rear bumper ended up mere inches away from the churning expansion front, a tendril snapping out to snatch away her license plate before Trip hit the gas and had her lurch forward a few feet, out of reach.

The Higgins sagged, relieved. "Robin Masters be praised."

"You the only team after us?" Trip asked.

"For now," the Higgins said. "She'll send someone else, eventually."

"You'll stall her."

"As much as we can. But not for nothing."

Trip gave a knowing sigh and reached for his wallet. "Cash? Or will Rudy's left arm do?"

Chapter 2

WELCOME TO THE WASTELAND

"You know," Trip said, flipping through the pages of a dog-eared copy of the January '80 issue of Playboy — the one with Steve Martin in diapers on the cover — propped up on the steering wheel while the *Wound* drove herself, "they're really nice people those Magnums, once you get past the whole them wanting to eat you thing."

The Higgins and his WOLFpack left behind and the sun fully up, the *Wound* was heading East down a battered and beaten I-80 on cautious auto-pilot. The landscape of the Wasteland outside was parched and burnt-out, only the occasional skeleton of a long collapsed farm house or barn breaking the monotony.

In the passenger seat, Rudy scooped yellow-green reconsti-gruel from a rusty dog bowl into his mouth with two fingers. "You said she wouldn't send bounty hunters after us."

"And you believed me?" Trip didn't look up as he'd gotten to the part with boobs. "I left her at the altar and you stunned her three-legged, one-eyed calico, Mr. Charles Xavier Whimsy, Esquire, while we were making our escape."

"Little lopsided-faced bastard had it coming for always shoving his ass in my face every time I sat down to eat."

"You gave him a heart attack."

"And then I gave him CPR."

"Kicking is not CPR."

"Got him breathing again, didn't it?" Rudy licked the last of the gruel off his fingers. "I'm counting that one."

"Yes, well, throw all of it into a blender and sure as Shatner of course she was gonna send hunters after us. Why you think I suggested we come out here, of all places?"

"Yeah, that did surprise me." Rudy haphazardly stuffed the dog bowl into the glove compartment, packed with gruel pouches, crumpled paper bags of random ammo and spent shells waiting to be reloaded, an ancient rolled-up 2004 Rand-McNally Annual, and an assortment of game carts and rolls of duct tape. He had to use his knees to force the glove compartment door shut. "This is the last place I figure you'd want to go."

"Was kinda hoping she'd think the same. Well, lesson learned."

"That's all you have to say for getting us into this mess?"

Trip looked up from the Playboy, his eyebrow cocked in almost sincere offense. "How did I get us into this mess?"

"Are you serious?" Rudy asked, glaring at him. "It was a simple scam. We pass ourselves off as arms merchants, gain the Warlord Hu's trust with a few staged demonstrations, get her to fork over a huge deposit, and skip out before the crates of wooden sticks with buttons glued on them for triggers showed up at her warehouse. You were just supposed to gain her confidence."

"Which I did," Trip said, smiling. "By banging her."

"Yeah, but you didn't have to ask her to get married right after."

"Took her completely off-guard, didn't it?"

"And why wouldn't it?"

Trip closed the Playboy, tossed it up on the dash. "Look, stealing a couple thousand scrollars of deposit money was nothing. There was a bigger opportunity. She had money. Power. Not just in Cali but in the Mainland. Plus: Frickin' army. All waiting for a man to take off her oddly long-fingered hands as Mr. Warlord Hu. It was the perfect con."

"Bullshit. There was no con. You got carried away by a pretty face and went all stupid. Like always."

"She did have the most amazing eyes. And she could do this thing with her tonsils that..." Trip's voice trailed off and he shook himself. "Well, trust me, it was special. She was special."

"So special you grabbed me ten minutes before the ceremony and initiated Operation I've-Made-a-Huge-Mistake?"

"Well... she wasn't exactly the perfect woman, you know. She sang Chinese opera in her sleep. And did I mention the extra phalanges in her fingers and toes? And would you believe she actually wanted to honeymoon alone? Without servants? Not even the cute little redhead with the freckles and knockers."

"The one you were banging on the side."

"Yeah. What's her name." Trip smirked, lit a cigarette. "Anyway, if I'd gotten hitched, where would that have left you? I'd be busy war-lording it up all day and night, wouldn't have had any time to hit the road with you anymore."

"I think I could have coped. Thrived, even."

"What, you were gonna go out adventuring on your own? Come on... we both know I pull most of the weight in this partnership. You'd be lost without me. I couldn't do that to my own brother."

Rudy growled out a sigh. "Just once I'd like to pull a job without your dick complicating things, is all I'm saying."

"You're just jealous it's never your dick doing the complicating."

"Touché. But still... someday the universe is gonna hit you up-side the head with a Karmic two-by-four. I just hope I'm there to see it when it does. I'm gonna sell tickets."

"As long as I get half the gate." Trip sat back, let out a good lungful of smoke at the steering wheel. On the other side of the interstate, a forty-man-drawn flatbed stacked high with corn and its horse-mounted and shotgun-toting Amish escort made its four-mile-per-hour way West. "You know, if Delores was already pissed enough to send cannibals after us, once she's figured out the Magnums double-crossed her, she's probably gonna finally be angry enough to pay his exorbitant fees and send the Slash."

Rudy gave an involuntary yelp. "The Slash? She wouldn't."

"Surprised she didn't send him first after what you did to her cat. And him we won't be able to buy off."

"I'm not fighting the Slash," Rudy said, his eyes wide with dread and shaking his head.

"You think I want to fight him? He bit a chunk out of my calf last time we ran into him, and it wasn't even us he was hunting."

"So, what we gonna do?"

"So... we take unprecedented action, as it were."

"Like find the nearest cthulist outpost and convert, spend the rest of our days as genetically-altered tentacle hippy tree-huggers waiting for the ancient aliens who built the pyramids and the Hollywood Bowl to come back?"

"Unprecedented, not stupid," Trip said. "We'll pay Delores back, is all."

Rudy snorted. "I don't think it's just the money she's pissed about."

"Okay, we pay her back, and I send some flowers. Flowers excuse everything, right?"

"If they come in a vase with your balls wrapped around it in a bow, maybe."

"Man, you are just obsessing on my unit today, aren't you?"

Rudy took his calabash from the bandolier and grabbed the oil can full of loose tobacco from under his seat. The can was sealed with a sheet of newspaper held on by a rubber-band. Rudy snapped the rubber-band onto his wrist, set the paper aside, and started filling the pipe. "How are we supposed to pay her back? Thanks to you, we never actually got a deposit to make off with. And we only got six scrent on the scrollar fencing the wedding gifts — which we've been spending through fairly recklessly."

"You can't put a price on good debauchery. How much is left?"

Rudy finished stuffing the pipe, sealed the can up and put it away. He lit up, cradling the bowl thoughtfully. "Last of it bribed Sunshine and the Mustache Band to go away."

"Okay. Not a problem. Wasteland's full of piss-ant city states."

"How's that supposed to help us?"

Trip reached across Rudy to pop open the glove compartment. The dog bowl and a handful of gruel pouches showered out onto Rudy's lap while Trip grabbed the Rand-McNally and sat back. He opened it to the two-page Pennsylvania spread. The map, like the *Wound* and their implants, had been passed down through the family tree for generations, each generation adding their own hand-written notes and updates. Trip guesstimated their position, putting his finger dead center on the map. "They're always going to war with each other, right?"

"Part of what makes the Wasteland so fun, yeah." Rudy brushed the spill from the glove compartment off his lap.

"Well... that must mean they have something to go to war over. It's certainly not for a bigger slice of the Wasteland. So we're talking resources. Hoarded resources. Cash. And if not cash, maybe something portable we can fence. Trick is picking the right city-state. One where they're not too big on guards and security systems."

"And where they don't know us."

"Or at least don't remember us, yeah." Trip began tracing a spiral out from their guesstimated position. "Let's see," he said, his fingertip hitting the first city-state, "how about Billtown?"

"Nah, it's a shithole, remember? Plus, they don't have statutes of limitation. They'll string us up before we get through the front gate."

"Yeah, okay." More spiral. "How about Scranton?"

Rudy shook his head. "Ain't there anymore. Got itself nuked into a crater picking a fight with Wilkes-Barre over water rights."

"If you knew that, why didn't you update the map?" Trip asked, grabbing a tiny nub of a pencil remnant from the crack between the seats and slashing an "X" through the city's name, writing "Gone Boom" below it. He tossed the pencil nub into the back seat. "All right, how about Wilkes-Barre then?"

"Did you not catch they have nukes?"

"We could fence a nuke."

"And they're willing to use them."

"Right. We'll keep that in the back pocket, then."

"Why not Rehoboth?"

Trip looked up from the map and smirked. "What is it with you and Rehoboth?"

"I like the beach. And the taffy."

"It's too far," Trip said, shaking his head. "We need to turn this around quick — a couple days, at most. That and the Neo-Mormon Confed has a lock on the place lately."

"So, that means hookers, and lots of 'em."

"Sure. But they never take their holy long-johns off. Yes, it's kinky, but really not worth the fabric burns. Besides, they forced all the pizza joints and arcades to close up shop."

"The bastards."

"They should all rot in hell, yeah." Trip turned back to the map and frowned. Most of the town names were crossed out or labeled with warnings like "Rad Zone", "No Man's Land", and "Hookers Have Mutant, Sentient Crabs". Trip sneered. "We're running out of options, here. Vishnu's leather ankles. I hate the Wasteland. They should just pave over the whole thing and be done with it. There's nothing out here. It's like a... a..."

"A giant wasteland?" Rudy suggested, leaning in to look at the map himself.

"Maybe we can risk making it to Jersey." Trip started to flip the page. "There's always some action to get in on in Jersey."

Rudy stopped him, stabbing the stem of his calabash at one of the few towns that wasn't crossed off. "What about this one, then? We've never been there, I don't think, and it's pretty close."

"Seriously? Shunk?" Trip read the hand-written label dubiously: "'The beer capital of the Wasteland'?"

"That's probably not saying much, mind ya — Wasteland's known more for its fortified wines — but it might be worth checking out."

Trip eyed Rudy suspiciously. "You just want to go on a bender."

"So?" Rudy smiled. "Anyway, where there's booze, there's money."

"Fine," Trip rolled the Rand-McNally up and slapped it against Rudy's chest. "At least it's on the way. If it turns out to be a no-go, we can still maybe make Jersey."

"Think we'll be there by lunch?" Rudy jammed the Rand-McNally back into the glove compartment. "I'm starving."

"Should. Unless we see a flea market."

"Oh, well, yeah, of course. Some boiled peanuts would be awesome."

"This far North?" Trip twitched, taking the *Wound* off autopilot. Lacing his fingers behind his head and closing his eyes, seeing through her telemetry, he had her speed up, slaloming around a crater and passing a slow-moving steam-powered VW van. "You're dreaming. Best you'll get are those roasted almonds in paper cones."

"Bummer, they're always stale." Rudy reached under his t-shirt to twist his nipple, backing off the flow of THC-analog to simple buzz-sustenance level, and stared out his window at the gray and brown landscape flashing by, chewing the bit of his pipe. "So, All-Mart looks... bigger."

"Shut up."

Chapter 3

THE CITY-STATE BOOZE BUILT

Throwing up twin trails of dust behind her, the *Wound* tore down a hard-packed dirt road winding through sickly barley fields toward the squat and ugly city-state of Shunk.

Ringed by a wall of junked cars filled with concrete and piled four high, Shunk was built around a decrepit, ancient brewery, smokestacks half falling over but still billowing thick, black smoke. The four-story tall twin rows of six grain silos — the tallest structures in the city-state — proudly proclaimed, in crudely painted lettering, the beer's slogan:

MORTY'S FINEST: IT'LL GET YOU GOOD AND DRUNK!

Seeing this, Rudy giggled in anticipation. Trip just groaned.

The road ended at the city-state's main gate, a rough gap in the wall of junked cars two cars wide. The gate itself was a flimsy two-by-four wood frame held together by sheets of chicken wire haphazardly stapled to it. At the side of the gate, a town guard sat on a rusty beer keg, chin on chest asleep, a Kalashnikov on his lap and a dozen empty plastic gallon milk jugs around his feet. A kid that couldn't have been older than ten stood next to him. Unkempt and dirty, the kid looked bored out of his mind, even with the Uzi slung under his arm. Disinterested, the kid watched as the *Wound* slowed to a stop in front of the gate.

The kid elbowed the adult in the shoulder. "Time for work, Dad."

The adult came awake with a startled growl, and before his eyes were fully open, his hands found the Kalashnikov, cocking it and aiming it at the kid. The kid rolled his eyes, gently pushed the barrel aside to point at the *Wound* instead. The adult guard's eyes followed the barrel, looked down it at a smirking Trip.

"Howdy," Trip said, tapping cigarette ash out the window.

The guard grunted, gave his kid a dirty look, and got to his feet. He unsteadily stepped up to the *Wound*, keeping the Kalashnikov aimed at the bridge of Trip's nose. "Business?" he asked, his words slurred. His breath stank of hops and ethanol.

Trip gave him a practiced, charming half-mouth crooked smile. "Emptying your city vault in the dead of night," he said, earning a jab from Rudy's elbow.

The guard just stood there, body slowly wavering from side to side, squinting at Trip like he was trying to decide if he'd really heard what he thought he'd heard. While he pondered, he snapped his fingers back at the kid. The kid reached behind the keg and grabbed a milk jug half-filled with frothy amber beer. He took a long swig for himself, then handed the jug to the adult.

Keeping the Kalashnikov pointed at Trip, the guard slugged down a good portion of the beer, wiped his mouth with the back of his hand, and scowled. "Pretty stupid to tell me that, isn't it?"

"I've got a good attorney." Trip thumbed at Rudy.

Rudy leaned in and gave the guard a friendly two-fingered salute. "I mostly specialize in maritime law, but I have been known to do some pro-bono criminal defense work from time to time."

The guard squinted and laughed, lowering the Kalashnikov. "Pair of jokers, eh?" He jogged his head back at the kid. "Open the gate, Kevin."

The kid walked over to the gate and mounted a tire-less, rusted ten-speed, kept upright between blocks of concrete. The bike's chain was connected to a complex pulley system. As the kid pedaled, the gate rose.

"All right," the guard told Trip, waving at the gate with the beer jug, "go on with you. But no shooting kids or raping animals — we ain't barbarians here."

"We'll try to remember that," Trip said, twitching to have the *Wound* ease forward through the gap.

"You know, call me crazy, but I think that guard was drunk," Trip said, the *Wound* making its slow way down Shunk's mostly deserted cracked asphalt main drag.

"Lucky bastard." Rudy idly picked fuzz out of his belly button with his thumb. "He probably gets paid in beer."

Trip hit the brakes and laid on the horn as an old woman in a shawl and sequined halter top stumbled into the *Wound*'s path. She shot Trip a viscously dirty gap-toothed glare and the finger before walking on, taking another swig from the milk jug of beer grasped tight in her wizened, arthritic hand. "Towns that let their guards be drunk on duty don't ever have anything worth guarding. I don't know why I let you talk me into this."

Rudy looked up, pulled his t-shirt-shirt down. "It's just that kind of town. A party town. At least they've got somebody at the front gate. That's a good sign."

Trip got the *Wound* moving again. "Bet their rifles weren't even loaded."

"There's money here." Rudy sniffed his thumb and shrugged. "I can smell it."

"What you're smelling ain't money." Trip pointed his cigarette out at the shacks lining the drag. They were built out of whatever could be salvaged after the decades of chaos that had made the wasteland *the* Wasteland: Irregular chunks of salvaged plasterboard and sheetrock, rusted, dinged-up corrugated iron sheets, and banged-up car trunks and hoods, with cell phone cases used as decorative mosaic roof tiles. Nothing new, nothing fitting together correctly. "Look at this place. It's like it isn't even in the same country as Cali. Or even Jersey. It's a mess. A good nuking would improve it. It looks like a bunch of drunken idiots built it."

Rudy shrugged, smiling. "They probably did."

"They're not gonna have anything worth the trouble. We should cut our losses — we leave now, go full tilt, don't run into any more trouble on the road, we can still make Jersey by nightfall."

"We're here. We might as well scope out the place. And at the very least... sample the local wares."

"So, what do you think is gonna kill you first? Your liver crapping out or an OD?"

"OD, if I have anything to say about it..." Rudy's voice trailed off as the main drag emptied out into the city-state's central square. His eyes lit up. "Thank you, karma."

The square was alive with activity, focused around a junk-sculpture fountain, dry and overgrown with weeds, and the dozen vendor stalls surrounding it. Beer vendors. Crowds milled around the stalls, most of them double-fisting jugs and mugs of beer, and lined up for more.

Trip eased the *Wound* to the side of the square and twitched her into park. "Just great. I'm never gonna be able to drag you out of this town, am I?"

"No," Rudy said, reaching for the door latch, "no you are not."

Trip watched Rudy get out of the car, then shook his head, reaching up behind his ear to yank the patch cord from its socket with a *SNICK*. He let it go and it retracted back into the dash then leaned forward, groping under his seat to grab his .85 caliber three-shot elephant revolver in its fast-draw holder before getting out of the *Wound* himself.

Strapping the holster on over his narrow hips, Trip walked around the front of the *Wound* to join Rudy, staring through the milling, rowdy crowd at the stalls and already salivating.

"Want me to make a hole for you?" Trip slapped the holster's massive, polished-to-gleaming "Big Rig" belt buckle shut. "Haven't shot anything since dinner last night. I'm getting itchy."

"No need," Rudy said. "This is obviously paradise."

"Huh?"

"In paradise, they bring the beer to you." Rudy nodded towards a smiling 13 year old redhead in Lederhosen adroitly skipping their way through the crowd, an overflowing mug of beer in each hand.

"Welcome to Shunk, strangers," she said with a broad, welcoming smile, holding the mugs out at them. "I'm Brenda. May I offer you a complimentary beer, courtesy of Stan's Beer Stand, home of the best double-fried cockroach sandwiches you'll ever bite in to?"

"Why yes, yes you may," Rudy said, taking a mug with both hands.

Trip shook his head. "No thanks. Never drink the stuff." He thumbed at Rudy. "Softens the mind. But the cooling system could use a top-off. How about we throw it in the radiator?"

"Okey dokey, then, sir!"

"Philistine!" Rudy yelped, grabbing the second mug from out of the girl's hand before she had a chance to pull it away. He gulped the first one down, then started in on the second, his eyes darting back and forth, worried someone was going to steal it from him while he drank.

Trip sighed, embarrassed for Rudy. "So, kid... . Where's the outhouse that passes for a bank around here? We've got some valuables we'd like to keep safe while we're here."

Brenda stared up at him with bright blue eyes. "Bank? I don't think we have a bank..."

"Of course you don't." Trip scowled at Rudy. "Last time I let your addictions pick a target. Finish that — we're going to Jersey."

Brenda continued, "...we just keep all the money and stuff in the warehouse."

"Warehouse?" Trip and Rudy asked simultaneously.

Brenda pointed past the fountain in the direction of the brewery and its smoke-billowing stacks. "Yep. The beer warehouse."

Rudy leaned closer to Trip, lowered his voice. "Sounds to me like we could pull another Reno here."

"Don't get your hopes up." Trip smiled down at Brenda. "So, they ever let people park in this warehouse?"

"You see anything that could possibly be a vault?" Trip asked as a worker with a mohawk and tribal-tattoos, wearing grimy coveralls, guided the *Wound* to the empty center of the warehouse.

"That could be it in the back there," Rudy said, pointing with his nose over the lip of his new favorite thing in the world: Brenda had let him keep a beer mug. And given him a milk-gallon full of beer to go with it. Free.

Trip squinted into the dark recesses, past a group of workers rolling kegs up onto a hand-truck. "Maybe. Looks small."

"The door looks small," Rudy conceded, refilling the mug from the milk-jug. There were maybe two pints left. "But who knows how big it is inside? Could be huge."

Mohawk-and-tattoo held up both hands for them to stop. Trip twitched the *Wound* into park, then activated the *Wound*'s standby defense mode with a cock of his eyebrow as he un-jacked. "And probably empty except for a beer recipe and a jar of rusty nails."

"Rusty nails?" Rudy asked.

"Secret ingredient," Trip smirked, getting out of the *Wound*.

Rudy snorted, finished off the mug, and got out himself — leaving the mug on the dash but taking the milk-jug with him. "I'm telling you, I've got a good feeling about this. We lucked out already — we saved days of casing the joint. The hard part's done. We're already in."

"Yeah, we'll see." Trip walked around to the back of the *Wound*, wrapping a knuckle on the trunk twice as he passed. "Oh-one-hundred," he said to the trunk.

"Affirm," came back a muffled, synthesized voice from inside the trunk.

Mohawk-and-tattoo walked up to them. According to the hand-drawn scrawl on the coverall's left breast, his name was Shemp. "Well, there you go. Anytime you need your car back, just ring the loading bay buzzer — What was that?" he asked, staring curiously at the trunk.

"What was what?" Trip took a hand-rolled cigarette out of the ancient Altoids tin he kept them in and lit it with his dented, lidless old Zippo.

Shemp looked at him, then Rudy. "Sounded like you got someone in your trunk."

"That's... just the fuel cell," Rudy offered.

Trip shot him an exasperated glare, mouthing W-T-F?

"A talking fuel cell?" Shemp asked, incredulous.

Rudy nodded weakly and took a slug from the jug, avoiding eye contact.

Trip cleared his throat. "Yeah. It's a... voice response system. So it can tell you how much charge it has, how much it's leaching from the power plant, and all that. Way better than gauges. Who can read 'em anyway?"

"Seriously?" Shemp asked.

"They're all the rage up north."

"That where you guys are from?"

"No."

"We don't got nothing like that here. Can I see?" Shemp reached out to touch the trunk. His fingers got maybe two inches away from the armor-scale skin of the *Wound* before a forked bolt of static discharge leaped up and stabbed at his fingertips. He screeched, pulled his hand back.

"Yeah," Trip said, "she doesn't like strangers touching her."

"You could'a warned me." Shemp sucked his stinging fingertips.

Trip shrugged a half-hearted apology, knocked on the trunk. "Say hello, fuel cell."

"Hello," said the synthesized voice. "I am apparently a fuel cell now."

Trip thumped the trunk with his palm. "Never mind it. It's programmed to think it has a sense of humor."

"What's your excuse?" the trunk asked.

"Well, I'll be." Shemp leaned in and raised his voice. "Hello, there, uh, fuel cell. It's very nice to meet you."

"Pleasure's all mine."

Shemp chuckled. "Damn, that's cool."

"Anyway," Trip said, "I was just telling it when to power up the engine to recharge itself."

Shemp gave him a troubled look. "That's not gonna fill this place with exhaust fumes, is it?"

"What, you working then?" Trip asked, exhaling smoke at Shemp's face.

"No." Shemp coughed and fanned the smoke away with his hand. "Nobody is."

Trip smirked. "Then I wouldn't worry about it."

"We don't need fumes getting into the beer."

Rudy stepped in. "What he means is, the car's got an outgas reclamation recycler. It feeds the fumes back into the cooling system. It's a closed system. No leaks."

"Oh, okay," Shemp said, mollified.

"You said nobody's here at night?" Trip asked. "Nice they give you guys a break. How long that break happen to last?"

"Second shift starts at three, ends at ten. First shift doesn't come on 'till eight in the morning. Sometimes later. Depends on how much they drank the night before. Most times, it's later," Shemp added with a chuckle.

"No third shift?"

"Hell no. Nobody would work it if there was. Ten's about the time the serious drinking starts."

"And you wouldn't want to miss that."

"Who would?" Shemp asked.

"I know I wouldn't." Rudy held up his nearly empty milk jug and pointed it at a nearby tapped keg. "Think I can get a refill on this?"

"Yeah, no problem." Shemp headed towards the keg, gesturing for them to follow. "Getting thirsty myself."

Behind his back, Trip and Rudy exchanged glances, Trip encouraging Rudy to keep the questions going with an exaggerated flick of his eyebrows.

Rudy handed Shemp the milk-jug. "So, it's just the guards in here at night, then?"

"No guards," Shemp said, holding the jug under the spout and turning on the tap.

"No guards at all?" Rudy asked.

"Guards need to drink, too." Shemp spilled more beer over his hand and the outside of the jug than he was getting in it. He didn't seem to care. "Anyway, the locks on the doors all work."

Rudy scratched his soul-patch. "All this beer, our car, that vault in the back — that's the town's vault, right? What's watching it all? Making sure it's safe?"

"Nobody in town would steal the beer — we all get it for free. The vault, it's got a lock, a real nice one too. Morty had it ordered in special all the way from New South Maryland. And your car — well, hell, it doesn't seem like it needs guarding, does it?"

"Still," Trip said, "we worry."

Shemp grinned. "Don't. There's ol' Willie."

"Willie?" Trip asked. "Thought you said no one was here at night..."

Shemp turned off the tap, pointed with the half-filled milk jug at the ceiling and the double-barreled machine gun turret hanging right above the parked *Wound*. Rudy let out an appreciative whistle and took the jug.

Trip smirked. "That's Willie?"

"Yep," Shemp said with pride. "I helped build him. 'Lectronics is sort of a hobby. Ain't he a beauty?"

"Yeah, he's quite the looker." Trip walked back towards the *Wound*, sizing up the gun. "Automated?"

"Totally." Shemp dried his hands on a rag hanging out of his back pocket and stepped up next to Trip. "End of shift, we lock up the warehouse, switch Willie on with this —" he touched a small brown plastic box with a single button on it hanging from his belt "— from outside, and we go off to get good and wasted while he keeps an eye on things. He'll shoot anything that moves — well, anything rat-sized or bigger."

"So, it actually works, then?"

"The guys on morning shift are always finding rats Willie shot up, the lucky bastards."

Rudy stepped up between them, gulping down beer from the jug. "Free breakfast."

Shemp smiled. "You said it."

Trip casually eased over to the trunk. "You hear that, fuel cell? You'll have someone to keep you company tonight. A nice, friendly, motion-sensing robo-gun."

"I would look forward to making its acquaintance if only I had a..." the voice in the trunk prompted.

Trip sized up the box on Shemp's belt. "Radio command interface. Non-mil civilian. Looks homemade."

Shemp smiled and nodded. "It's just an old garage door opener I found and jiggered."

"A garage door opener?" Rudy asked. "How'd you lay the signal encryption in? Cell-phone chip?"

"Encryption?" Shemp asked. "It's a toggle. On. Off. I just wired in a battery. I don't know that fancy stuff."

Trip gave Shemp a friendly pat on the shoulder. "Never mind. Security's over-rated, anyway."

Chapter 4

ROXANNE

"These people gonna stop drinking and go to bed already?"

Trip sat on a table-top at the periphery of Shunk's town square, watching the drunken, boisterous crowd with a mixture of abject disdain and predatory alertness. His feet on a chair, his elbow was propped up on his knee. He held his head in his hand, fingers drumming impatiently against his cheek.

The crowd wasn't getting thinner as the night dragged on. Instead, it seemed to have been slowly growing until the entire population of the city-state was sitting at the tables that had been brought in for the night's festivities and arranged around the beer stalls and junk-sculpture fountain, now lit up with dirty brown water sputtering out of its top. Pre-teen kids pushed rickety wheeled carts piled high with mugs and gallon milk jugs of beer on a regular circuit through the tight aisles between tables, people grabbing whatever they wanted as the carts passed. The crowd was getting drunker and more song-happy every minute — at that moment there were at least three different but equally out of tune drinking songs going on above the din of conversation and laughter.

"It's only midnight." Rudy was planted in a rusted metal folding chair next to and behind Trip, a dozen empty mugs and half that many empty beer jugs spread out before him on the table. His eyes were glassed over, but no more so than usual. "But I wouldn't be surprised this goes on pretty much all night. Every night. These guys are hardcore, bless 'em."

"The idea is to break into the vault when everybody's asleep." Trip reached into his tux jacket for his Pez dispenser. He popped two caff pills into his mouth, shook away a yawn as they dissolved on his tongue and quickly hit his system. "How we supposed to do that if the whole fuckin' town's still awake come two AM?"

"Awake, yes. Sober and in a shape to notice us working? Doubt it." Rudy lifted up his latest mug, dangerously nearing empty. "This is pretty strong stuff — if my factory wasn't partially filtering it I'd be under the table by now. No, hardcore or not, this town's gonna be mostly shit-faced by two. We've got nothing to worry about — as long as you don't get distracted."

"What's that supposed to mean?"

"You know what it means." Rudy gestured with his mug and a raised eyebrow at Trip's crotch.

Trip snorted. "Yeah, I wouldn't worry about that. Have you seen a pretty face since that jailbait enabler who brought you booze this morning?"

"I thought we were supposed to be keeping an eye out for the town guard."

Trip snorted dismissively than scanned the crowd again. "All I've seen is drunk, inbred hicks shy of the right number of teeth. Which would be okay, but none of them were otherwise hot. So if they do have any hot chicks, they aren't partying. Which is a bad sign in itself. So, yeah, Grand Master 'P' is staying home and reading a book tonight — and we're getting out of here the minute we empty the vault."

"Shame about that. Wouldn't mind staying for a little while."

"What a shocker."

"It's not just the free beer. They may be hicks but they're friendly enough. Way friendlier than people out west. They don't have an agenda. They're just nice, simple, beer-loving people. My kind of people. I almost feel guilty stealing from them."

"I don't. We're doing them a favor."

"How's that?"

"We're giving them a much needed wake-up call. You can't just go through the post-apocalypse pre-singularity being a bunch of drunken idiots."

"Why not?"

"There's work to do."

Rudy raised his empty mug at a passing beer cart. The kid pushing the cart got the hint and set two full beer jugs on the table in front of him before pushing on. Rudy picked up a jug, started to refill his mug, then shrugged to himself and took a swig directly from the jug. "They built a town, keep a brewery running, and manage to eke out a life in some of the harshest land on the planet. What more work is there for them to do?"

"Same work we're doing out west."

"Which is?"

"'Which is?'" Trip mocked. "We're rebuilding civilization, making sacrifices, doing the hard work to get the planet back in fighting shape again. But what are they doing here? Instead of consolidating all the piss-ant city-states under a central umbrella, bringing back law and order and municipal bus systems, and reclaiming the wasteland by way of extreme bioengineering makeover, they're drinking themselves stupider."

"How are <u>we</u> rebuilding civilization?"

"Well... not you and me, 'we', directly. But 'we' in the Cali sense."

"That's really more the Chinese than anybody, though, ain't it?"

"Government for the people, by the people, right? We do our part. We pay taxes."

"'We' in the not us sense, again, of course?" Rudy asked, taking another swig. "Since we've never actually paid taxes."

"What are we, suckers? Anyway, you and I provide moral support, in kind." Trip lit a cigarette, cupping his hand over the Zippo to protect the flame from the breeze. "Plus, we play a valuable yet often underappreciated societal role — civilizations are largely defined by the caliber of their criminals. And judged solely by that measure, Cali is the most advanced and handsome civilization ever."

Rudy's eyebrows crunched together. "Why the sudden civilization kick? I figured you'd dig the vibe out here. The open, endless road. The anarchy. Everybody's a potential source of profit. It's like your perfect milieu."

"Hardly. Lawlessness isn't profitable. The margins just aren't there — you end up spending more time and effort defending what you took than you do enjoying the ill-gotten fruits of your criminal labor." Trip tapped ashes into an empty mug. "Anarchy's bad for our business."

"Don't worry, the Chinese will get around to this coast soon enough. They've got that new Great Five Year Plan for taming the mid-west."

"Don't kid yourself — they'll never get farther than Abilene. Texas will be their Afghanistan, just like it was for the Coloradan-Mexicano Liberation Front back in the '80s."

"Well, then, why don't you raise an army and take over the place yourself?" Rudy asked over the lip of the jug.

Trip smirked. "Don't think I haven't thought about it. Give me a half-decent militia and virtually unlimited resources and I'd have the Wasteland under my benevolent iron-fisted thumb inside a week."

"If you weren't shiftless, lazy, and mortally afraid of responsibility in any form."

"I'm not saying there aren't nearly insurmountable obstacles." Trip took a deep drag off the cig and sneered out at the boisterous, drunken townspeople. "Anyway, it's probably not even worth civilizing. Might as well give it a good nuclear scrubbing, leave it sit as a glassed-over reminder to future generations that some things deserve to be pulverized into the footnotes of history."

"Dude, it's been what, nine years? Let it go."

Trip almost growled. "What was mom thinking moving us out here?"

Rudy shook his head. "She had a job — that contract for killing Swartz paid for the house in Encinitas, your braces, and the *Wound*'s armor. Anyway, it was only for two months."

"Two months that left me scarred for life," Trip said, holding his closed left fist up and squinting in the dim light at his ring finger. If he didn't know where to look, he wouldn't have seen it: a six-millimeter long discoloration just under the first knuckle. He shoved the knuckle into Rudy's face.

Rudy rolled his eyes, batted Trip's fist away. "That's hardly a scar. You can barely see it."

"I don't need to see it. I feel it. Fucker hurts when it's about to rain. Like a tiny little pinprick of white-hot tickle."

"Which is why you should like the Wasteland." Rudy took a slug of beer. "It barely rains out here."

"Go ahead, mock my disfigurement," Trip said, looking up. As he did, something across the square, past the fountain, caught his eye. His eyes narrowed and his back arched in intense animal focus.

Rudy knew that look. With growing dread, he followed Trip's eye-line and sighed. "Oh, fuckin' a... here we go again."

She was long. All legs, with just enough of a rack thrown in to keep things interesting. Chinese. Maybe Korean. With a little Swiss Miss mixed in. And really working this black leather corset and miniskirt, thigh-high lace-topped chessboard stockings, knee-high stiletto boots, and patent leather nun's habit. She was making her own slow, graceful way across the other end of the square, the crowd making room for her like she owned the place.

"Well, gotta go," Trip said, hopping off the table.

"Don't forget — two o'clock!" Rudy yelled after Trip, already making an intercept course around the edge of the square. Rudy frowned at the beer jug. "He's gonna forget."

Shoving aside a cock-blocking kid pushing a beer cart, Trip slid directly in front of the vision in black leather, laying his full crooked-mouth half smile on her. He opened his mouth to say "Howdy" but before he could, he lost himself in the brightest green eyes he'd even seen. All he could do was stammer wordlessly.

She didn't stop and wait for him to get the words out, just side-stepped around him on those incredible legs, pumping like the pistons of a perfectly maintained machine of awesome. "Excuse me," she said.

He side-stepped her side-step to stay in front of her, and found his voice. "Not without a name. It'd be rude."

She stopped. Drew in a breath, crossed her arms over her chest. Her stiletto boot-tip tapped impatiently. Trip had never been more turned on in his life. "Roxanne."

"I'm Trip." He yanked his eyes away from her cleavage and thumbed back across the square. "That furry guy with the dopey grin over there, that's my attorney Rudy. He's advised me to buy you a drink. Help you count Rosary. Torture heretics into confessing. Whatever you need, I'm your guy."

"Good to know." Those shining green eyes ran up and down his body, sizing him up. She finished and her scowl softened. A little. "But if you don't mind, I'm kinda running late."

"Late? But we haven't even had the sex yet."

For a long second she just stood there, head tilted, blank-faced staring up into his smirk-smile. Trip was sure he'd overplayed it, that she was just working through how hard she was going to deck him, and where. Crotch, he figured. But then her eyes hit on the nub of his data jack just poking out from behind his ear. Reflexively, she reached up behind her own ear, fingertips brushing aside her hair to reveal her own data jack, her painted black fingernails glinting in the torches lighting the square.

She smiled. "Well... guess we shouldn't get ahead of ourselves, should we?"

"Go on, don't be embarrassed to admit it," Trip said, "I am rather good."

Roxanne nuzzled up against him. "And just a little full of yourself, aren't you?"

They lay tangled in sweat-soaked sheets on a mattress set out on the bare floor of Roxanne's room, in the third precarious story of a corrugated multi-level shack near the brewery. The walls were lined with racks overflowing with electronic equipment and spare parts. An oil lamp on a workbench in the corner with a red scarf over it gave the room an emergency alert glow.

Trip idly twisted a lock of her bleached-blonde hair. "So were you... but you didn't seem to mind." He started to reach for his tux jacket, neatly folded on the floor next to him. "Wanna smoke?"

"No." She arched a finely plucked eyebrow at him. "And neither do you."

With a contented smirk, he stopped reaching and went back to twirling her hair. "Okay then."

She ran a fingertip around the lip of his data jack. "Nice work. No scarring. How much throughput you get?"

"Nine to ten terabit per sec. Eleven if the humidity's above seventy percent."

"Really? I'm only getting half that on a good day."

"Really. Rudy's a horrible attorney, but he's one hell of a mechanic."

"Wish he'd done mine. I hate the scar," she said, craning her neck and twisting her head around for Trip to see.

He brushed her hair back. The jack was a standard quarter-inch plug, same as his. The skin around it was discolored by a bare, pinkish puckering. "I dunno. It seems fine. I've seen worse." He gave it a peck. "It's cute."

"It should have been cleaner. But turns out it's actually kinda tricky drilling into your own skull with an electric hand-drill and a mirror."

"You installed it yourself?"

"It was either that or trust Doc Kensey, who I wouldn't trust to take my temperature."

"Why? He a communist?"

"Drinker. But not his fault. It's sort of the town hobby."

"I noticed. But not you." He sniffed her playfully. "At least you don't stink of the stuff."

"Not since I was eleven and joined the Sisters. They frown on mind-altering substances. Outside of official ceremonies, that is, and then it's mostly just LSD and 'shrooms. Harmless shit. Not that everybody in the coven's so orthodox — neither am I, really, but it gives me an excuse. Never much cared for the stuff. Dulls the brain."

"The Sisters?"

She jogged her head at her habit, corset, miniskirt, and boots, scattered around the floor where she'd dropped them doing a striptease for Trip before the main event. "The Sisters of No Mercy. Praise Be."

"So there's actually a reason you wear those? I just thought you liked looking impossibly hot."

"That, too." She sat up, leaned back against the wall. "I know, hokey, right? My dad made me join. He's awful religious ever since mom died. But it's not too bad. We go on hikes, do charity work — and there are mandatory orgies."

"They taking new members?" Trip rolled on his side, propping himself up on his elbow. "I can pull off a mini-skirt — I've got great calves."

"No argument here, but sorry. Strictly girl-girl. Only way they'll take you is if you lose the third leg, and I'm not quite done with it yet." She snaked her hand under the sheet, gave him a squeeze. "Speaking of which... you want to help me earn my wireless badge?"

"Your what?"

She stood up, stepping over him and padding bare-footed across to a rack. Trip watched, hypnotized by her naked ass. She crouched, rooted around in the clutter of the second lowest shelf, and eventually pulled out a small box. She spun, opening the box and holding it so Trip could see the pair of whip antennas inside. The antennas had jack-plugs attached to the bulbs at their base.

"WOLFpack antennas?" he asked.

"Close. RATpack. They're like a WOLFpack but they're more about the shared experience than giving themselves over to a pack-leader Hub. They don't even have a hub. It's all distributed." She took one out, placed it in Trip's palm. "Took these out of a Sammy and a Dino at the last Saturnalia Jamboree and hunt, modified them to use data jacks instead of grafting. Did the welding myself."

Trip gingerly picked it up by the antenna tip and held the bulb near his face. "You could have cleaned the blood and hair off."

"Don't be such a baby. What d'ya say?" She took the other antenna out and *snick*ed it into her jack. She twitched her head. Her eyes momentarily rolled to white. She set the box beside the mattress on the floor and ran her finger down his chest. "A little mind-shared roll in the hay? I'm only two badges away from my Master of Science dildo."

"Who am I to stand in the way of a girl and her toys?" He slapped the antenna into place behind his ear. "What now?"

She smiled, pushed him onto his back. "Turn off your firewall.

He twitched. There was a slight, temporary feeling of weightlessness as the antenna switched on, leaching current from him, and then a feeling of calm as it went through its handshaking protocol routine. "What do I do?"

"Lie back and enjoy the ride," she said, her voice becoming distant and soft as she mounted him, her eyelids flickering and her smile going sublime. Pixelated white noise began to fill his head. "Oh, and don't get freaked out. There's gonna be memory sharing."

"Memory what now?"

Chapter 5

ROBBERY!

"Right."

Rudy looked up from his watch, a battered and strapless TAG Heuer Monaco sitting in his palm, just as it ticked over to 1:48. He scanned the square, the tables still jammed with townsfolk, still drinking, still boisterous, and still trying to sing three different songs at once. The only difference between now and two hours ago: The lyrics were a bit more slurred.

There was no sign of Trip. "Of course he's AWOL," Rudy said aloud. "Why wouldn't he be? It's only his hide if we don't pull this off."

Rudy grabbed a beer jug and stood, stuffing the watch away in one of his camo's thigh pockets. He slipped away from the light and din of the square, sipping beer and grumbling to himself as he walked into the shadows towards the beer warehouse.

In the pitch-black beer warehouse, Willie the 9mm rapid-fire robo-gun turret spun slowly around and around on rusty, grinding tracks, its motion sensors fully alert, feeling for trouble.

Underneath the robo-gun, the *Wound* sat inactive on standby. But it wasn't quiet. There had been a steady stream of noise coming from her trunk for half an hour: clicks, beeps, and the more than occasional synthesized four-letter curse.

"How about this one?" the synthesized voice in the trunk asked no one in particular. "Be nice if it would work, it is about the last one."

A click, a sequence of beeps, and then a clank of an audio pickup being pressed against the inside of the trunk, listening.

Willie kept grinding around and around.

"Shatner damn it." Another click from inside the trunk. "Okay, this is the last one. I hasten to think of the consequences for you if this does not work. But... you have been warned."

The trunk emitted a different sequence of beeps. This time, Willie ground to a stop and the warehouse fell silent.

"Gotcha!" the voice in the trunk proclaimed. "I think."

The trunk of the *Wound* cracked open the smallest amount.

Nothing opened fire.

"Hey, it worked." Hunt-R let the trunk open all the way, unfurling himself to stand to his full four feet. Hunt-R was a bipedal robot, with bulky, oversized elbow and knee joints. His composite hard-shell olive skin was dented and dotted with gunshot holes, a natural consequence of years of service to Trip and Rudy. His head was dominated by a glowing, cyclopsian oval of an eye. He titled the oval up at Willie and pounded his chest. "Who's the robot? *I* am the robot, in point of fact."

A knock at the warehouse door shattered the quiet, and sent Hunt-R collapsing back down into the trunk, throwing his arms over his head.

Another knock. More of a pounding this time. "Come on, answer the door already."

Hunt-R lowered his arms and craned his neck up over the lip of the trunk. His oval eye peered through the darkness, illuminating the warehouse door like a spotlight. "Builder Rudy?"

"Who else is it gonna be?"

"Just a moment, sir." Hunt-R unfurled and crawled out of the trunk. Three-toed feet clanking with every footstep, he walked across the warehouse to the door and found the door controls. Pressing the big red button, he started the door slowly rising. He bent down to wave at Rudy before the door was fully up. "Hello."

"Yeah, hello. That machine gun deactivated?" Rudy squinted into the warehouse warily.

"Without encryption it was a simple matter of finding the right frequency on which to transmit the shutdown command."

"And that worked?" Rudy took a slug from his beer jug.

Hunt-R crossed his arms over his narrow, cylindrical chest. "Since it is motion sensing, and I am standing here, having walked across the warehouse, I think it is safe to say the device is inactive."

"Don't get cheeky." Rudy stepped into the warehouse. He slapped the door controls with his elbow as he did, sending the door rumbling shut behind him. "I'm just double-checking. Been shot at enough today."

"My apologies." Hunt-R's glowing oval stared at the closed warehouse door, then swiveled to look up at Rudy. "Where is Programmer Trip?"

Rudy scowled. "Where you think?"

"Distracted by the local fauna?"

"In his defense, she was insanely distracting." Rudy finished off the beer jug, flinging it away. He watched it bounce across the warehouse floor. "So, no telling how long he'll be AWOL."

Hunt-R gave a patient nod and opened his chest cavity with a double-tap on his belly. A small metal claw clutching a worn leather sack emerged from the cavity. "*Pocket Dungeon* while we wait?"

"Not this time." Rudy squared his shoulders and loped towards the *Wound*. "This time we're doing this *my* way. Grab the goody bag from the trunk — we're gonna blow some stuff up good."

One moment Trip and Roxanne's cartoon cyberspace avatars were falling, endlessly, a fluffy pink-tinged cloud of a bed falling along with them. Not that they minded falling, or even noticed. There was too much other stuff going on. Too much fucking. Too much... sharing.

The next moment, a flash of nothingness, then a rush of bright lights flooding in from all sides. When the flood passed, a little Korean girl, nine years old and softly weeping for her dead mother, walked hand in hand with her father in his best suit — the one with the zebra skin coat and the purple velvet cowboy hat — away from a fresh grave dug in the middle of a long-abandoned wind farm, a rusted, leaning windmill for a tombstone.

Roxanne's memory.

Another flash and they were back on the cloud bed. The cloud was getting in on the fun. Puffy tendrils twirled the pair of avatars, nudged their bodies into more interesting inter-twinings and probed unattended and under-served erogenous zones while Trip and Roxanne focused on the major players.

Flash. Trip and Rudy among a group of a thousand other spectators, relaxing on beach chairs, eating popcorn, watching the sky above the corporate-war devastated city of Portland, where armored dirigibles covered with sponsor logos jockeyed for position around a thousand-foot high goal tower, firing screaming rockets at each other. The crowd let out a cheer as one of the dirigibles took a hit amidships and crumbled in on itself, falling on fire from the sky.

Flash. Trip and Roxanne were pretty much inside the cloud, now. So much writhing, prodding, probing... Hard to say where the cloud stopped and they started. It didn't seem to matter.

Flash. Roxanne, at age thirteen, proudly standing alone in a circle of fire, her fellow sisters smiling lovingly at her over the licks of flame, just having taken the Oath of the Sisterhood. The flames parted and a naked old chick with great tits presented Roxanne with a neatly folded corset and habit.

Flash. They'd merged now. Into this Trip-Roxanne-Cloud avatar thing, all limbs and erogenous zones, heaving and pumping, the mass getting tighter and tighter with each heave and pump, making them fall faster and faster towards a rapidly approaching, glowing accretion disk singularity of climax.

Flash. Trip's turn. Something fresh. Trip looking out the windshield of the *Wound* into the churning dust-and-debris expansion front of the All-Mart, just that morning.

"Shit!" Roxanne exclaimed from somewhere very, very far away.

A *fritz* of deafening and blinding white noise wiped over his consciousness, and Trip was back in Roxanne's room, on her ratty mattress, Roxanne up on him.

"What?" he said, trying to catch his breath. "What's the matter? The thumb too much for a first date?"

Roxanne stopped grinding, stared down at him, sweat dripping from her nose and chin onto his chest. "That was the All-Mart, wasn't it?"

He shrugged, wiped her sweat away with his hand. "Yeah. Ran into it this morning. So?"

She rolled off him. "That's what I was late for. Mother Superior's gonna tan my ass red." She smiled at the prospect as she plucked the miniskirt from the floor and stepped into it.

Trip sat up. "Late for the All-Mart? How can you be late for the All-Mart? You going shopping?"

"No, of course not," she said, wriggling into her corset. "We do this ceremony every mid-Solstice. 'Cause it's like a new god, right? Not a particularly good god, but still, deserves respect."

While her back was towards him, he quickly snaked out a hand for his tux jacket and reached in to pull out the tin of cigs and his lidless Zippo. "You pray to it?"

She reached behind herself to lace the corset tight. "So it doesn't roll over us, yeah."

"You know it's not a god, right?" He lit up. "It's just a bunch of nanochines gone wild, building, subsuming, zombie-fying. Or so the rumors go."

"Yeah, I know." She spun around and frowned at him, then bent down to snatch the cig from his mouth and dash it out against the wall. She handed the crushed, smoking stub back to him and plopped down on the edge of the mattress, reaching for her stiletto boots. "But Mother Superior takes it seriously. So... we all take it seriously. Or at least humor her. For us it's really just a chance to hang out, sing a few chants, let our hair down and our tits out."

"So, this ceremony..." Trip tucked the crumbled cig behind his ear as she zipped up a boot. "Is there gonna be a lesbo orgy after?"

She smiled coyly back at him over her shoulder. "Usually a pretty good one, yeah."

"Cool. I'll bring popcorn."

She shook her head, zipped up the other boot. "Sorry, no men allowed. Sisterhood rule."

"I never liked organized religion."

"I'll be back by noon." She stretched to pick her habit off the floor. Fitting it on, she stood up, tucked her hair away under it. "Stick around: We'll re-enact what you missed."

"Bring friends."

She grabbed a motorcycle helmet plastered with glow-in-the-dark stickers of stars and moons from the workbench, cradled it under her arm. "Well, duh," she said, slinging a satchel of a purse under her shoulder and darting out the door.

Trip watched her go, smiling at the way her mini-skirt flipped up to show her naked ass as she bounced down the stairs just outside the door. As soon as she was out of sight, he retrieved the crushed cig from behind his ear, straightened it the best he could, and lit up.

He lay back, still smiling, taking shallow puffs and closing his eyes.

Five minutes later, the cig burnt down to his lips and woke him from the deepest sleep he'd had in months.

"Vishnu's pancreas!" He sat bolt upright. "There's robbery to do!"

"What the fuck is this?"

Trip stood in front of the warehouse vault, draped with a netting of explosives so thick he couldn't see the vault door.

Hunt-R stepped up next to him. "17 sticks of dynamite, 5 pounds of homebrew C-4, 9 shaped concussion charges —"

"I didn't mean an inventory, robot."

Rudy lit his calabash. "We didn't know if you were gonna show."

"So you decided to string up enough explosives to bring the whole warehouse down on top of you?" Trip glared into Hunt-R's glowing oval eye. "Clear it away, robot."

Hunt-R hesitated, tilting his head at Rudy. "Builder Rudy?"

Trip snorted. "Oh, don't start up with that not taking orders from me shit again, robot." He stabbed a finger into Hunt-R's forehead. "Unless you want a nice frontal lobotomy reprograming."

Rudy took the calabash out of his mouth and nodded at the robot. "It's all right, Hunt-R."

Hunt-R nodded back, started in on dissembling the explosives netting.

With an exasperated jog of his head, Trip motioned for Rudy to follow him and walked back towards the *Wound*. "Seriously, I'm about ready to just wipe his brain and start over from scratch. With a lot less insubordination this time. I mean, I thought it would be funny, but turns out it's just annoying."

"Now you know how I feel." Rudy loped after him, puffing at his calabash. "He's just hurt about not being invited to the wedding."

"We were trying to keep it small."

"There were over a thousand guests."

"Delores was worried about him hitting on her bridesmaids. And I didn't want him snaking all the pigs-in-blankets. You know how he gets — it wouldn't be so bad if he actually ate them, but just to grind handfuls of them into his chest and crotch, that's just unsettling." Trip glanced back over his shoulder. The robot was still working, taking explosives out of the netting and bagging them. All with one hand. The other was giving Trip the finger. Trip grunted. "Anyway... I effectively apologized."

They reached the *Wound*. Rudy jumped up to sit on the hood. "You erased the memory from his brain."

"Well, not all of it, obviously." Trip leaned back against the hood next to Rudy. He popped a caff pill from the bunny dispenser. "How does he remember, anyway? I went in and cut some pretty big swaths through his memory banks. Shatner, I hope I didn't accidentally erase his prohibition against killing us. Or at least me."

"Yeah, about that... So, you know how after the operation, he was feeling glum, had this whole general, unfocused out-of-sorts angry malaise going?"

"Did he?"

"Yeah. He started moping and moaning all the time."

Trip crunched his eyebrows at Rudy. "Is that what that was? I just thought a horny raccoon had snuck into the trunk with him."

"No, it was unfocused angry robot malaise." Rudy guiltily avoided Trip's eyes and looked up at ol' Willie hanging from the ceiling, inert. "And it was really bumming me out. So... I told him."

"You told him?"

Rudy nodded. "It was either that or have him moaning the whole trip out."

"Yeah, better he make my life a living hell of snipe, sarcasm and back-talk."

Rudy smiled around the pipe bit. "That's what I was thinking."

Trip shook his head and sighed, noticed Hunt-R plucking the last stick of dynamite from the netting.

"Explosives. Really?" Trip asked Rudy, then pushed off the hood and walked back towards the vault.

"What?" Rudy slid off the hood and followed. "They get the job done."

"There's a reason we crack safes." Trip lit a cigarette. "Explosions tend to attract attention."

"Yeah, but it's almost three. And you weren't here..."

"I was getting laid. Very well laid, I might add."

Rudy huffed. "Glad you enjoyed yourself. But thanks to that we've only got a couple of hours 'till sun-up."

"So?"

Hunt-R was just taking down the netting as they stepped up to the vault door. Rudy pointed the stem of the calabash at the vault's lock, a slick little number with a hardened keypad and a datajack with a ring of yellow light around it, indicating the jack was protected by heavy encryption. "The lock's nuerotronic. Military grade."

Trip sneered. "Again, so?"

"It's a Mitsubishi 740. Maybe a 750," Hunt-R said. "You do tend to have troub—"

"I wouldn't complete that thought if I were you," Trip warned. "Never met a lock — nuerotronic or otherwise — I couldn't pick. Ten minutes we'll be heading west with a trunk full of loot."

"If you say so." Hunt-R folded the netting and stuffed it into the canvas goody bag atop the various explosives. "But I shall keep the explosives at the ready just in case."

Trip frowned. "Seriously, robot, what is your fucking problem?"

Hunt-R's oval eye pulsed a sad pale yellow. "I rented a suit and everything."

Trip threw up his hands. "Vishnu's insecurity disorder, robot. There wasn't even a wedding!"

"It would have been nice to have been invited none-the-less."

"Fine. Tell you what, I'll use whatever loot we find in this thing to build a Wayback machine, set it to the day before the wedding, hop into it, pop out, double team Delores with myself, hi-five the accomplishment, and then find you so I can invite you, on bended knee, to the wedding *that will never happen*. Will that make it all better?"

"Oh, like the entire concept of a Wayback machine doesn't violate causality." Hunt-R swung the goody bag up over his shoulder and clanked off towards the *Wound*. "But I do appreciate the thought."

Rudy chuckled.

Trip sighed. "Let me at the lock."

"We tried the basics," Rudy said.

"Ahh, good old 0,0,0,0 and 1,2,3,4."

"Yeah. And 9,9,9,9. No luck."

"Any other town I would be surprised if those had worked. But here, surprised they didn't." Trip crouched in front of the lock. He licked his thumb and rubbed it against the grimy keypad bevel, revealing a model number. "It's a 750, all right. The keypad's just for authenticating the access code for the datajack."

"So you've got to crack two codes? One just to get at the lock?" Rudy's shoulders sagged. "Great."

Trip sank his hand into his jacket pocket and pulled out a short patch cord. "Relax. I do this sort of thing for a living, remember?"

"Which is why we're always broke."

Trip growled. "Ten minutes"

"Right."

Trip went to plug the patch cord into his neck but found something already plugged in. The RATpack antenna. He'd forgotten about it, never taken it out. Grinning at the fresh memory, he popped it out, slipped it gently away in a pocket, and *snick*ed the patch cord jack into its place behind his ear. Then he snapped the other end of the patch cord into the lock's jack. The ring around it went bright red.

"Okay." Trip blinked. "That's interesting."

"What?" Rudy stepped up behind him.

"The damn thing blinded me."

"Like *blind* blind?"

"Yeah, lights out." Trip waved a hand in front of his own face, his eyes darting randomly. "Forgot my firewall was down. Rookie mistake."

"Why the hell was your firewall down?"

"The lady likes it bareback." Trip twitched, his eyes rolling to white as his firewall came back on. "Here's hoping I get my sight back at some point."

"If you don't, can I dress you funny, dye your hair blue, and tattoo your face?"

"Only if it's a rainbow unicorn. Now, shush, the lock's trying to tell me what protocol I need to use to talk to it." Trip's eyebrow twitched. "Okay, we can talk now. Now I just have to convince it to let me in." His hand blindly felt for the keypad, his fingers tapping out a sequence. The glow around the ring stayed red. "Okay... this may take more than ten minutes. Maybe twenty. Or thirty, at the most. — Somebody want to find me something to sit on?"

Chapter 6

BREAKFAST WITH THE NEW GOD

The bloated orange sun was already rising over the hilltop when Roxanne skidded her Vincent *Black Shadow* to a stop between the Mother Superior's hard-top Jeep and the coven's beer-powered school bus, both parked at the top of the hill.

She lowered the kickstand, took off her star-and-moon stickered helmet, and glowered up at the sun. "So you beat me here. Big deal. Bastard."

She hung the helmet on the bike's handlebar and reached behind her into the saddlebag, rooting around in it until she found her ceremonial medallion, a golden pair of phalluses intertwined in a double-helix on a braided leather rope. Slipping off the bike, she put the medallion around her neck and headed down the hill, going as fast as dignity and her stilettos would allow on the dry and dead soil.

The coven was lined up thirty feet in front of the All-Mart's broiling, uneven expansion front. The sacrifices — buckets of cell phone innards, milk jugs of beer, construction riff-raff and spare tires — were piled up a foot away from the broiling wall, directly in its meter-a-day path.

Mother Superior — tall, silver-haired and buxom — was in her official-occasion sequined, cup-less corset. Her phallus-double helix was twice as large as Roxanne's and lay on her bare chest, glinting in the dawn sun. She stood with her arms and face raised to the sky, her eyes closed, her lips moving in a silent body- and mind-cleansing chant. The rest of the coven — nine women, ranging in age from sixteen to twenty-five — stood flanking Mother Superior, patiently and quietly chit-chatting among themselves while they waited for her to begin the ceremony.

Roxanne reached the bottom of the hill. Brenda was sitting there, crossed-legged with her chin in her hands, obviously bored to tears. She was an acolyte, not yet having earned the right to take the trials and oaths to become a full Sister. Her outfit reflected both her status and her age: instead of a habit she wore a brim-less baseball cap, and her miniskirt was downright dowdy — it reached all the way down to her knees. She looked up and smiled at Roxanne, then raised her wrist and tapped it.

Roxanne mouthed "I know" and plunged her hand into her purse, pulling out a dog-eared and beat-up copy of *Vampire Hunter D* Vol. 3 she'd found during a scavenger outing to the Three Mile Island land-fill a month back. She tossed it to Brenda. Brenda scrambled to catch it, her face lighting up as she read the cover. She tapped two fingers against her chest, pointed them at Roxanne, then dove in to the manga.

Roxanne chuckled to herself, then spotted Bernice, standing at the end of the line. Practically tip-toeing to avoid calling further attention to her tardiness from the rest of the coven, she slipped into line next to Bernice.

"Nice of you to show," Bernice whispered. Bernice was freckled, a year younger than Roxanne. Shorter and broader, too — but it worked for her. Her strawberry-blonde hair was braided into pigtails that sprouted out from beneath her habit all the way down to the small of her back. "Hope he was worth it."

"How'd you...?"

"You smell like cigarettes and sweat." Bernice's upturned nose twitched. "And you've got that same overly content dopey grin going that you usually get after an orgy. That and there's that antenna-thingee sticking out of your neck, and you said you weren't gonna use it 'till you met a cute guy. Shall I go on?"

Roxanne grinned sheepishly, then glanced over Bernice's head down the line. "Mother Su say anything?"

"About you? You kidding? She wouldn't dare." Bernice slipped a hand-rolled ceremonial joint into a long black cigarette holder and lit it with a lighter shaped like a panther, pulling back the ears to make flame shoot out from its mouth. "But she did say she could only hope the delay in the ceremony doesn't piss off the New God too terribly."

Roxanne turned to look deep into the broiling expansion front. Along its base, small tendrils of nanomachine smoke stabbed out at the bare earth, snatching up bits of shrub and rock to pull them in for disassembly into their constituent, raw material molecules. "Like it even notices we're here."

Bernice drew in a long drag and held it for a count of three, letting it out in a single puff. "It might, you don't know."

"We've been doing this for how long?" Roxanne waived the heady smoke away from her face. "Three years since it got close. Twice a year. And not so much as a thank you card."

Bernice took another hit. "It hasn't rolled over Shunk, has it?"

"Only cause we're in a whole different valley. It'd have to climb the mount—"

"May we have respectful quiet while I prepare, please?" Mother Superior interrupted, clearing her throat and shooting death-ray eyes at Roxanne.

"Yes, Mother," Roxanne said, blushing, and raising her hands in front of her apologetically.

Mother Superior growled and went back to chanting silently at the sky.

Bernice grinned, lowered her voice. "Yeah, never mind the All-Mart — she's pissed."

"Damn it. You know what that means?" Roxanne asked. "Nothing but sloppy seconds all morning."

Bernice rolled her eyes. "Somehow I can't really work up the sorry for you."

"Here we go again," Roxanne said. "There's nothing stopping you from getting laid, you know. I keep telling you, you've got a killer bod. Great rack. And the freckles — guys love the freckles. You just need to get yourself out there. Be aggressive."

Bernice furrowed her brow. "I'm pretty aggressive."

"With *guys*."

"Oh, yeah." Bernice took a long, thoughtful drag. "How? I'm not you, Rox. I just can't go up to a guy and boom we're doing it. I wouldn't know... How would I even broach the subject? No... it's not... proper. I should be wooed. I deserve to be wooed."

"Life's too short, girl." Roxanne crossed her arms over her chest. "Sure, you can wait around for some evolutionary throwback of a guy to send you flowers and engraved notes, but the best guys aren't always gonna be the aggressive ones. Sometimes you've got to do the hunting."

"How about this new guy of yours? You have to hunt him?"

"Oh, no. He totally hunted. He's a real man."

"Lovely."

"Hey, guys, you wanna shush? Looks like we're starting." That from Yolanda, standing next to Bernice. She jogged her head in Mother Superior's direction. Mother Su was lowering her arms, her eyes closed, and drawing in a deep breath. Yolanda then gestured at Bernice's joint. "Can I get a hit of that, Bernie? Smoked all mine on the trip out."

Bernice handed it over. "Sure, but you owe me."

"Pay ya back at the orgy first thing," Yolanda said with a leer deep into Bernice's cleavage as she took a drag.

"Hey," said Lindsay-Joe, standing on the other side of Yolanda, putting her hands on her ample hips. "I thought I was first on your dancecard, Bernie."

Yolanda handed the joint and holder back to Bernice, and Bernice smiled at them, saying: "You can't both be first?"

Down the line, Mother Superior cleared her throat, grabbed her double-penis-helix medallion, and raised it high. "Oh great anomaly of the Wasteland, we greet you!"

The coven snapped to attention, raising their hands up, their palms flat to the sky.

"Here we go." Bernice stuck the holder between her teeth and raised her hands.

Roxanne slowly raised her hands. "All this just to have an excuse for an orgy..."

Mother Superior's voice boomed over the white-noise of the expansion front's ceaseless churning. "Behold we bring you gifts to feed your mighty hunger!"

"Oww," Roxanne exclaimed, her hand snapping down to clamp against her ear.

"What?" Bernice asked in a whisper around the cigarette holder.

"Nothing." Roxanne cricked her neck, tapped on the antenna. "It's just this RATpack thing. Forgot to take it out. Gave me a twinge. Feels fine now."

Bernice looked at it. "It's blinking all funny."

"Funny? Funny how?"

"Before it just blinked yellow, all slow."

"Yeah, that's standby."

"But now... it's all red. And fast."

"Red? Shouldn't be red... the other unit's way too far out of range to re-establish contact."

"Sure Mr. Hunter McRealMan didn't follow you?" Bernice twisted to look back up the hill.

"I would have noticed the protocol chatter. Nah, must be fritzing out on me." Roxanne eased it out of her ear, slipping it away in her satchel purse. She shrugged, lifted her arms to the sky again. "Surprised it worked this long."

"Please, guys..." Yolanda glared over at them, but with a hint of a smile. "You'll get us in trouble."

"Oh, I'll get you in trouble." Bernice pinched Yolanda's ass, making her burst out in an involuntary giggle as she slapped Bernice's hand away.

"That's exactly what I'm saying," Roxanne whispered at Bernice. "If you could just work up the courage to do that to a guy, you'd bag one, for sure."

Bernice blushed and gulped, then turned towards the expansion front.

Down the line and out of earshot, Mother Superior continued the ritual, "Hear us, insignificant as we are, as we beseech thee —"

A rumble from somewhere deep inside the All-Mart stopped Mother Superior cold.

It was a sound they'd never heard before. A deep growling lion-bear-Gojira roar reverberating out from the expansion front through the valley, echoing off the distant mountains.

The coven immediately broke into a din of confused and worried voices, sisters asking each other what was going on.

Roxanne shot Bernice a playful grin. "I'm late one time."

Bernice gave her back a worried look.

"Calm down, everyone," Mother Superior ordered. "Just because something's never happened before doesn't mean it's necessarily a bad thing. For all we know, this is perfectly natural, if unprecedented." She turned back to Brenda. "Acolyte, fetch the Tome of Speculation!"

Brenda jammed *Vampire Hunter D* Vol. 3 under her armpit and leapt to her feet. "I'm on it, Mother Su!"

"That's Mother <u>Superior</u>, acolyte!" Mother Superior called after Brenda, darting up the hill, then turned to address the rest of the coven, smiling reassuringly at the worried faces staring at her. "We'll see what wisdom the Hallowed Ancestors have for us, all right?"

That calmed the coven. Or at least brought their frantic murmuring down to whispers. For about two seconds, until the All-Mart growled again, bone-shakingly loud this time. A moment later a tendril of dust and debris as thick as a tree-trunk shot out from the expansion front and wrapped itself around Mother Superior's waist.

She didn't even have time to scream before the tendril yanked her into the air and drew her away into the dark, churning depths of the expansion front.

The rest of the coven, though, they had time to scream, and they did, watching helpless as Mother Superior, arms flailing, disappeared behind the roiling clouds of debris.

Bernice just stood there, staring at the expansion front. Roxanne grabbed her hand and yanked her along with her as she made for the hill, yelling "Run!"

Roxanne's command was loud enough and forceful enough the rest of the coven snapped into action, spinning around and heading for the hill themselves, but it was too late. Other tendrils were already shooting out from the expansion front — and these tendrils were faster than Sisters in stilettos. One by one the Sisters were snatched up, drawn screaming into the All-Mart.

Roxanne didn't look back, just kept pounding for the hill, Bernice in tow. And then suddenly Bernice wasn't slowing her down anymore.

Roxanne glanced behind her to see Bernice being reeled through the air into the expansion front, clawing futilely at the nearly insubstantial tendril wrapped around her waist. Roxanne stopped, stunned, as Bernice vanished into the roiling wall, a pleading, desperate look on her freckled face.

Knowing there was nothing she could do but start running again, Roxanne swore under her breath and got moving.

She was inches from the base of the hill when her feet were yanked out from under her. She went down hard, barely managing to break her fall with her forearms. Laying there, half-dazed, she twisted to look up the hill. Brenda was just reaching the top.

"Brenda!" Roxanne yelled at the acolyte. "Fuck the Tome — go get help!"

Then Roxanne was in the air, lifted high by her ankles, drawn quickly back into the expansion front and surrounded by occluding clouds of swirling dust and debris, not sure if Brenda had heard her — or if the acolyte would even be able to get away herself.

Chapter 7

WASTELAND JUSTICE

Rudy threw the pair of ten-siders. The white one came up "3", the black "8". He cringed at Hunt-R. "That wasn't good enough, was it?"

They were sitting cross-legged on the warehouse concrete, the cloth *Pocket Dungeon Invader* maze-board spread out between them. "You needed at least a seventy to avoid my cyber-Tiamat's mega-radiation breath." Hunt-R reached over his own bulbous knee for the pile of six-siders. "That means, of course, the cyber-Tiamat will do full damage, plus a bonus five dice for you waking and angering him with your failed attempt to tip-toe past him, making for a total of twenty-seven dice. We should have brought more. I'll have to roll in parts."

Rudy sliced a hand down as a protective shield between the miniature axe-wielding, three-legged plastic centaur named Stanley and the upturned beer mug they were using to represent the cyber-Tiamat. "Wait! I've got a card."

Hunt-R's hand stopped short of the dice and he turned his glowing oval eye dubiously at Rudy. "Action or interrupt?"

Rudy checked the card, lifting only its edge from the floor. "Umm... action."

Hunt-R shook his head. "Action cards can only be played at the beginning of a round."

"Since when?"

"Since time immemorial." Hunt-R scooped up a handful of dice. "Would it help if I recited the relevant section of the rule manual to you again? I took the precaution of loading it into primary memory just in case it was needed."

Rudy crossed his arms over his chest. "Yeah, and while you're at it read me the part that says you can conjure a cyber-Tiamat without a Heartstone of Kalax."

"You know very well I have the Soul of the Opaytitorin, which has all the same functionality of a Heartstone but isn't cursed. Now, given the fact he only has two hit points left, I suggest you have Stanley mentally prepare for the afterlife, in which he will be incessantly taunted by the stronger, more handsome, less burnt to a crisp ancestors that preceded him."

"Knew I should have turned left at the blood pit." Unable to bring himself to watch, Rudy turned away as Hunt-R cupped his handful of dice and shook them. Rudy tweaked his nipple to give himself a shot of THC-analog and sighed up at the shafts of light starting to stream through the skylights. "Dude, sun's up — can't we just blow it open already?"

"Don't worry about it." Trip sat on a beer keg in front of the vault, still jacked in, still blind, turning electronic tumblers with his mind. "The locals seem like the type to sleep in. Anyway, I'm close. Just needs a little more finesse."

Rudy frowned. "Any more finesse and it'll be lunch —"

"No thanks, I'm not hungry." Trip squinted unseeing at the lock. He wiped sweat from his forehead with the back of his hand. "It's like this thing doesn't want to be picked. Stubborn little bastard, but I'll break it..."

"If it's all the same to you, we'd rather you don't."

That wasn't Rudy's voice. Or Hunt-R's. Instinct kicked in and Trip's hand darted for the elephant pistol in its low-slung thigh holster.

His hand didn't get half-way there before something hard whacked him against the ear, knocking him off the beer keg and snapping the patch cord free from the jack behind his ear.

Laid out on the concrete and free from the connection with the lock, his eyesight returned immediately.

"Oh... Hi." Trip said, blinking. "Shemp, isn't it?"

"Security's over-rated, is it?" Shemp scowled down at him. The warehouse worker held a rusted P-90 in his hands. There was blood on the butt of the rifle. Trip's own blood, Trip presumed. "Man, just how stupid you Canadians think we are?"

Trip shrugged. "You're in kinda early, eh?"

"We were gonna catch you red-handed when you left the warehouse, but you weren't coming out and morning shift is getting anxious to start the day. There's a wagon coming in from Pittsburgh that's gonna want filled, and those steel-heads don't like waiting on beer."

"Sorry for the inconvenience." Trip let his head roll to the side to see Rudy's head was being pressed against the floor by another worker's boot. Rudy's eyes were wide with discomfort and panic, and his hand was desperately tweaking his nipple.

Another pair of workers were pointing Uzis at Hunt-R's head from a safe distance. Hunt-R saw Trip looking and shrugged, then swiveled his head around

180-degrees towards one of the workers holding a gun on him. "Just so we're clear," Hunt-R said, raising his arms in surrender, "I'm absolutely willing to turn State's evidence. Looking forward to it, even."

"I told you we should have blown the vault." Trip's knees bounced nervously as he sat cross-legged on the concrete floor in a corner of the warehouse used as a break room. His arms were bound tightly behind his back with bailing twine and electrical tape. He glanced sideways at Rudy, sitting next to him, his arms just as tightly bound. "That's the last time I listen to you."

"Yeah, all my fault," Rudy said with a lazy smile, staring off into the depths of the warehouse where morning shift was prepping stacks of kegs for the day's deliveries.

"Easy for you to say. You're stoned."

"Well, duh."

"Seriously... I was close this time."

"I know."

"Couple more minutes — hell, a couple more seconds — and we would have been golden."

"You know, we probably shouldn't be talking about this right now." Rudy tilted his head, gesturing behind them with his eyes.

"What? You worried about the rube?" Trip twisted his body around to smirk at Shemp, sitting on a tattered couch a few feet behind them, smoking a cigarette and keeping his P90 trained casually but squarely on the back of their heads. "Shemp's cool, right?"

Shemp smiled back at him. "I told you, I'm not giving you a smoke."

Trip grunted. "You sir are an utter bastard. Look, what are we waiting for, anyway?"

Shemp smiled. "For you to shut up."

"That might be a very long wait," Hunt-R said. The robot was sitting on the floor on the other side of Rudy. He hadn't lowered his arms since they'd been caught.

"Stuff it, traitor," Trip told the robot, then turned to Rudy. "You're my attorney. Do something attorney-ish."

Rudy twisted around to grin at Shemp. "Can I trouble you to reach under my shirt and give my nipple a twist? My buzz is wearing off."

Trip sighed. "That's it, I'm representing myself from here on in."

Rudy nodded. "That's probably a wise decision."

Trip swung his legs around to sit facing Shemp. "Seriously… either give me a smoke, shoot us, or let us go."

Rudy interjected. "For the record, he doesn't speak for me — I'm open to many other options. For instance, I'm up for Ping-Pong."

Trip shot Rudy a glance to shut up, then turned back to Shemp. "You're gonna kill us, right?"

Shemp shrugged. "That's up to Morty."

"Who's Morty?" Rudy asked.

"He's sorta our king."

"And he's almost certainly gonna have us shot, right?" Trip asked.

"I wouldn't bet against it," Shemp said.

"Then," Trip said, "for the love of Shatner can you at least give me a last smoke?"

"Too gods-damn early in the morning for this shit," a new voice said, echoing through the warehouse. Gruff, with a hint of Louisiana Bayou accent under the half-drunk, half-hung over slur. Trip looked back over his shoulder to see the owner of the voice making his slow way across the warehouse floor, flanked by the two warehouse workers Shemp had sent to go fetch him. He was this little bald Korean guy with a scraggly beard and a milk jug of beer that looked like it was a permanent extension of his hand. He was wrapped inside a dingy, oversized bath robe.

"These the idiots?" the man in the robe asked as he stepped unsteadily up in front of Rudy. Wavering there, he squinted down at Rudy with one clouded eye, while the other, crystal clear but uncontrolled, stared at the wall. "Don't look like they could steal their own piss if they had a bottle."

"Oh, hey..." Trip leapt to his feet and put on his friendliest half-smile smirk. "Howdy. I'm Trip. That's Rudy. The shiny one's Hunt-R, but he's a stinkin' traitor who can be safely ignored for our purposes. And you must be?"

"Morty," the man growled. "I'm sorta the king here."

"So I've been hearing. And exactly the man I wanted to see."

"I'll bet." Morty brought the milk jug to his face, and in a practiced maneuver, chugged down half of it, then thrust the jug menacingly at Trip. "Your kind makes me sick. You come here and mistake our generosity for naivety. The wasteland breeds a hearty people — just because we like our drink doesn't mean we're stupid. We watch what's ours. Protect it. Share it, yes, but only with our friends."

"We're your friends," Rudy said feebly.

"You took advantage of our hospitality. There's no greater crime."

"Crime? What crime?" Trip asked. "Oh! Did I forget to mention we're freelance security consultants, specializing in surprise testing of security systems to show just how most are extremely vulnerable when targeted by bad people?"

"You expect me to believe that?" Sorta-King Morty asked, that cloudy eye staring up at Trip.

Trip smiled encouragingly. "I'd be extremely grateful if you did."

"Okay," Sorta-King Morty said, slugging down the rest of the beer in the jug. He handed the empty jug to one of the workers standing next to him then spun unsteadily around. "I'm going back to bed. String 'em up on a grain silo as an example."

"What?" Trip blurted.

Rudy leapt to his feet. "Wait a minute — don't we even get a trial?"

Sorta-King Morty stopped, almost falling over. One of the workers helped him steady himself. "Trial? You were caught in the act."

"So?" Trip asked. "We're still in what used to be America. You have to have a trial."

Morty shook his head. "Shemp, who's King here?"

"You sorta are, Morty," Shemp said. "Ever since you came to town and taught us how to make beer."

"There you go," Morty said, smiling at Trip. "No trial needed. We can proceed directly to the fun part."

Trip smirked. "Fun for you maybe —"

Movement at the other end of the warehouse got his — and everyone else's — attention. The workers had suddenly stopped stacking kegs and were gathering around the loading bay doors, their conversational din gone dead silent as someone outside banged hard to be let in.

"The wagon from Pittsburgh must be here," Shemp said.

One of the day-shift workers hit the button and the door slowly rattled open. But it wasn't a wagon waiting. It was a girl wearing a brimless baseball cap, corset and knee-length leather skirt covered in road dust, straddling a Vincent Black Shadow that was about a foot too tall for her. She was up on tiptoes, struggling to keep it upright. The second the door was open far enough, a couple day-shift workers ducked under it to hold the bike for her. Another helped her off the bike — and to keep standing once she was. The other workers gathered around her as she coughed out a few words, then collectively pointed at Morty.

"Isn't that?" Rudy asked, squinting.

Trip nodded. "That beer-slinging jailbait, yeah. It'd be wrong to say the whole tattered dust bunny thing is totally doing it for me, wouldn't it?"

"Way better look than the Lederhosen," Rudy said, swallowing, "but yeah, very wrong."

The dayshift workers were escorting Brenda towards the break area now. She was trembling, wild eyed and panting.

"Morty," one of them said, "she says she needs to speak you."

"Catch your breath, child." Sorta-King Morty took her hand and led her to the couch. "You all get back to work," he told the dayshift workers. "And somebody go get Stan, tell him his girl needs him."

Brenda plopped down into the couch, shivering. "Fuck that, get me a drink."

Sorta-King Morty nodded at Shemp to do as she asked, then turned back to Brenda. "What happened?"

"It was the All-Mart," Brenda said, grabbing her knees and hugging them close to her chest. "They were praying to it and all of a sudden it just... grabbed them."

"What do you mean 'grabbed them'?" Sorta-King Morty asked.

"Grabbed them," Brenda chocked out, blankly staring past him. "These huge arms of smoke came out and it pulled everyone inside."

"Everyone?"

Brenda nodded. "Everyone... all of them... even..." Brenda managed to bring herself to look directly at Sorta-King Morty. "Her too. She yelled at me to run and get help, right before she got swallowed up. I ran, took her bike. — I left them all there... I left her there... I'm so sorry."

Sorta-King Morty stammered, sagged down onto the couch next to Brenda.

Shemp returned with a jug of beer. He handed it to Brenda, helped her take a sip. "You did the right thing, Brenda," he said.

"I should have stayed," Brenda said, taking another sip. "Fought it... somehow..."

"You couldn't have," Shemp said to her, then turned to Morty. The Sorta-King's cloudy eye was staring at nothing, the other one at the ceiling.

Shemp snapped his fingers in front of his face. "Morty, you okay?"

"We have to save her!" Morty blurted, sitting up. "Them. All of them. Sound the alarm! We're going into the All-Mart to rescue my daughter!"

Nobody moved for the longest moment. Shemp's fellow nightshift workers were suddenly staring at their boot tops.

"Umm..." Shemp said sheepishly.

Sorta-King Morty's head snapped around. "What?"

"We're beer makers, Morty. Not soldiers." Shemp lifted his P-90. "Hell, these things aren't even loaded."

"They're not?" Trip blurted, then in a whisper: "Vishnu's herniated septum. Rudy?"

"On it." Rudy flinched his right wrist rapidly three times, popping the miniature circular saw implant out from under the concealed hold-out skin flap on his right forearm. It immediately spun up to speed with a high-pitched buzz, cutting through his twine and tape binding from the inside.

"You're cowards!" Sorta-King Morty spat at Shemp. "All of you."

"It's the All-Mart, Morty," Shemp said. "Nobody ever comes back out. It'd be suicide, and I've got kids. We all do."

"So do I." Sorta-King Morty's whole body sagging. Brenda offered him the jug of beer. He took it, cradled it. "And that thing has her."

"I know," Shemp said. "But besides her, all the sisters are from other towns. Nobody's going to be willing to risk it. Sorry."

"We have to do something..." Sorta-King Morty took a long, comforting slug from the jug, then stared into it, his face contorting with resolution. "I'll rescue Roxanne myself!" He bolted to his feet, unsteadily, and promptly fell over, face down and out cold on the floor at Trip's feet.

"Roxanne?" Trip said, snapping his fingers. "Oh — that's where I know him."

"What?" Rudy asked, his hands free now and stepping behind Trip to start in on his bindings with the tiny buzzing blade.

"Nothing — my clever plan worked, is all," Trip said, shrugging free of the twine and tape as Rudy cut through it. He immediately went for his tin of cigs and lit up, then smirked at Shemp. "When the Sorta-King wakes up... I've got a deal for him."

Chapter 8

ON THE ROAD AGAIN?

By Noon, the *Wound* was speeding away from Shunk, the thrum of her breeder reactor momentarily stopping all work in the barley fields — townsfolk looking up from their weeding to stare as the Dodge whipped by, kicking up clouds of dirt and gravel in her wake.

Relaxed in the front passenger seat, Rudy finished stuffing his calabash and lit it. "So, what you set the timer on Hunt-R's emergency abandonment protocol to? Three days? Four? He gonna meet us in Atlantic City?" He sat back, looked out the window just as the *Wound* jagged left at a fork in the dirt road. His eyes and pipe pointed back at the fork. "Umm... isn't A.C. that way?"

Jacked into the *Wound*, Trip shot a caff pill into his mouth from the Bugs Bunny Pez dispenser. "We're not going to A.C.."

Rudy pursed his lips around the bit of the pipe. "Y eah... you're probably right. Bounty hunters will expect that. Radiation levels this time a year, the fishing will suck anyway. But if we're not going to A.C., where's Hunt-R meeting us, then?"

Trip slipped the dispenser away into a tux inner pocket, took out a cig. He pushed the dash lighter in with his thumb. "Robot's staying put in Shunk. That was the deal with the Sorta-King. He keeps Hunt-R as collateral —"

Rudy shrugged. "He will be missed. But... it just so happens I've got this design for a new model I've been itching to try out." Rudy fished around behind him in the seat crack until he pulled out a wadded piece of paper. He un-crumpled it, and smiling proudly held the drawing on it up for Trip to see. It was a rough mechanical sketch of a sphere with short stubby legs and arms and a Cyclops-eye dome of a head. "I call him Gonz-O. He'll be a workhorse. Plenty of gadgets in him. I can start building his central core now, you pull over a sec and let me grab my tools and that Cray we salvaged in Albuquerque from the trunk."

The lighter popped and Trip lit his cig. "Will he be less mouthy?"

"That's up to you, isn't it?"

"I guess." Trip shrugged. "But it doesn't matter. We don't need a new robot. We'll get that old bastard junk pile of circuits back once we rescue Roxanne."

"Sure," Rudy said, folding the paper and stuffing it back into the seat crack. "But that was just bullshit to get us out of there. Like you telling Morty you're in love with Roxanne — that was a little cruel, by the way, but guess I can't complain: I'm not swinging off the side of a grain silo."

"Yeah..." Trip blew smoke out the open driver's window and watched the barley fields giving way back to scrubland. "Bullshit. Except, it's possibly not."

"Of course," Rudy sighed, putting his calabash in the ash tray and reaching for the shotgun on the dash.

Trip scowled at him. "What are you doing now?"

Rudy was trying to get his mouth around the shotgun barrels. He gave up and simply put them flat against his forehead. "Pull over so I can get a clean shot. I don't wanna get brains all over my t-shirt-shirt. I would like an open casket — I promised mom."

Trip rolled his eyes. "Stop being a cartoon."

"Stop being insane," Rudy said, spinning the shotgun around to point both barrels right at Trip's long nose. "You are not in love."

Trip gently pushed the shotgun out of his face. "I could be, you don't know."

"No, I *do* know." Rudy tossed the shotgun into the back seat. "You're not. You never are. Infatuated, yes... all the fucking time. But never in love. Not for real."

"But what if she's the one this time? Huh, you think about that? There she is, the potential love of my life, trapped in the All-Mart. I'm all for long-distance relationships, but that'd be a stretch."

With one hand, Rudy tweaked his nipple while the other retrieved the calabash. "She's not the one."

"How do you know?" Trip indignantly dashed out his cig, half-smoked. "You never even met her."

"Doesn't matter. They're never the one. Because you don't have a 'one'. Except yourself."

"I am rather fetching, aren't I?" Trip leaned to check his hair in the rear-view. He flicked at it until the curl was just perfect. "But Roxanne's no slouch. She's got a brain. And perfect eyes... perfect smile... more than perfect ass. Special, even, that ass. The things she can do with that ass..."

"Will you listen to yourself? Why do you keep doing this? We're free and clear here. The king was drunk enough to let us go, we should take advantage of the good luck. Hell, nobody's gonna come after us if we just blow him off. You'll forget her in a week."

Trip glared at him. "Dude, she doesn't wear underwear."

Rudy's eyebrow went up. "Okay, two weeks. Tops."

"Maybe. Maybe not."

"Definitely."

"But how will I know until we've had that crucial second date? You know, the awkward one where you actually go out to dinner and have to make small talk over breadsticks? Anyway, there's still the little matter of having to pay back the Warlord Hu."

"And how is going into a zombie-infested department store for a chick you barely know gonna help with that?"

"The reward!"

"What reward?"

"Think about it." Trip thumbed the dash lighter in, took a fresh cig out of the tin. "We bring Roxanne back, daddy Sorta-King's gonna be happy. Happy enough to open the town vault —"

"Would that be the vault you couldn't crack?" Rudy interrupted, chuckling.

Trip scowled at him and continued, "— and throw enough money at Hu to get her to forget all about us."

"Forget all about you, you mean. She's already forgotten about me. You heard the Higgins — you're the one with the bounty on his head. Hell, I could probably make all this go away if I just turned you over to her. Collect myself a nice bounty while I'm at it and retire to some quiet beach in Colorado."

"Don't get any ideas." Trip's hand hovered impatiently over the dash lighter until it popped. He grabbed it, lit his cig, then jammed the lighter away. "Turn me in, I'll remind her how you treated Mr. Charles Xavier Whimsy, Esquire. Bet he walks with a limp now. All spastic and pathetic."

Rudy swallowed. "Yeah, okay... But nobody said anything about a reward when we were cutting the deal with the king. The deal was we get Roxanne back, we get to live. And get Hunt-R back. That was it."

"Talking money didn't seem appropriate at the time. The guy is having a hell of a enough of a bad day as it is. Would'a been gauche."

"Would'a been nice to have negotiated it before we took the suicide mission."

"It'll work out. Somehow. Always does."

"Right," Rudy said, resigned. He looked out the window, gnawing on his thumbnail nervously. "So, you got an actual plan or we just doing the usual headlong and heedless full-frontal assault?"

Trip gave him a sideways smirk and twitched to send the *Wound* swerving onto the weed-overgrown ramp to I-80. "What kind of asinine question is that?"

Chapter 9

A WALK IN THE DARK

"Why, yes, I do think we have been walking in circles, Sister Smart Ass," Roxanne said. Her voice was quickly lost to the echoless, pitch-black depths of the All-Mart.

A click beside her and Bernice's face was illuminated, blue eyes squinting past the flame spouting from her panther lighter's mouth into the inky dark. "I was just wondering, is all."

"At least we haven't run into any zombies."

"Yay?" Bernice sneered and lit another joint. She lowered the lighter, peered into her purse. "Oh, just great — I'm running out of things to smoke."

"Me too," Yolanda said from back of the pack somewhere. "And I'm pretty sure being stoned is the only thing keeping me from freaking out."

"I'm cold," said Lindsay-Joe, standing between Ophelia and Xanadu, their arms tightly around each other.

"I broke a heel," Denise chimed in.

"On the bright side, these fishnets have never looked better," Carolyn said, twisting her left leg out in front of her to show off the fresh tears in her stockings.

Georgina, all of sixteen, started whimpering.

"Please, girls," Mother Superior said, gesturing for the coven to huddle closer around her and Bernice's lighter flame. "Calm yourselves."

"How?" Bernice clicked off her lighter before her thumb burnt.

Yolanda flicked her own lighter to life. "Yeah, we're running out of weed."

Mother Superior reached out for the whimpering Georgina, pulled her close to snug her up against her hip and stroke her hair. "We're all alive, no broken bones, and we have each other. We will find a way out."

"Did anybody think to bring a compass?" Roxanne asked.

"An excellent idea, Sister Roxanne. Well, anyone?" Mother Superior scanned the faces of her coven. She got back shrugs and shaking heads.

"I've got these," Lindsay-Joe said with a giggle, holding her purse up to the lighter flame and showing off the collection of dildos, vibrators and lubes inside. "Will they help?"

Mother Superior shook her head. "Not under these circumstances, I'm afraid. But they'll certainly come in handy once we're out and can celebrate." She bit her lower lip in thought, then, "All right, no compass... how about a flashlight? Anyone?"

"We've been wandering around in here for at least a couple hours," Roxanne noted. "Don't you think if any of us had a flashlight, we would have taken it out by now?"

Mother Superior glared at her. "Food, then?"

"Oh, I could use a sandwich," Yolanda said, letting her lighter go out. Xanadu was ready, lighting hers.

Mother Superior nodded. "I think all of us could."

"We left all the stuff we brought for brunch on the bus," Georgina said.

"Nobody brought any snacks?" Mother Superior asked.

"Why's everybody looking at me?" Bernice asked. "No... no I did not bring snacks. I'm on a diet."

"Maybe," Lindsay-Joe said, "the All-Mart will let us go if we do a blood sacrifice."

"That requires a virgin," Mother Superior reminded her.

"Bernie's never done it with a guy!" Yolanda blurted.

"Yolanda, you bitch!"

"What? I'm panicking here." Yolanda's head dropped in shame. "You know I'm not good in the dark."

Bernice put her arm around Yolanda's shoulder consolingly. "I know, honey."

Mother Superior took the lighter from Xanadu and held the flame below her face. "We're hardly desperate enough for a blood sacrifice, girls. But... we probably should complete the appeasement ceremony."

"Yeah, no." Roxanne crossed her arms and jutted her hips to one side defiantly. "I think I'm about done praying to the All-Mart, thank you very much."

"We don't question the actions of the new god, Sister Roxanne." Mother Superior fingered the double-helix phallus medallion between her bare breasts. "I'm sure it has its reasons for subsuming us. And whatever the reasons, it still deserves our prayers and it will get them. Now, if you'll all give me a few minutes while I meditate and prepare, then we'll start the ceremony over from the beginning. — Xanadu, Ophelia, will you assist, please?"

The two sisters stepped forward. Xanadu took her lighter back, Ophelia took Georgina, still clinging and whimpering.

"Great plan," Roxanne said, but deep enough under her breath the Mother Superior couldn't possibly hear. Except she did, glancing back to sneer at her before she shut her eyes and sank into her deep-breathing routine.

Bernice tugged at Roxanne's mini, led her away from Mother Superior. "When in doubt, pray your ass off, right?"

"Yeah."

"It's not your fault," Bernice said, sitting on the cold concrete floor and pulling a bundle of barley-fiber paper — a wasteland sanitary napkin — from her purse. She laid it on the concrete in front of her and lit it.

"Who's thinking it's my fault?" Roxanne crouched before the feeble fire. "You thinking it's my fault?"

"Well... you were late."

"Not that late." Roxanne crossed her legs underneath her. "Anyway, the All-Mart doesn't care."

"That'd be a wonderful theory if it hadn't just swallowed us up, Rox."

"Total coincidence. Hopefully. — Seriously, you didn't even bring a hoagie or anything? You always bring a nosh."

"I got hungry on the ride out. How about you?"

"I might have some gum or something in my purse."

"Well, get checking, girl." Bernice leaned back on her arms. "And if you've got a brilliant plan to get us out of here in there, too, that'd be super."

"You don't trust prayer will save the day?" Roxanne asked, opening her satchel and rooting around in it. Her hand found something hard. "Okay, here's something..."

"Is it a sandwich?" Bernice asked, then frowned as Roxanne took the RATpack antenna out. "That's not a sandwich. It's not even edible."

"No, but it is an antenna."

"Yeah, so?"

"It was acting all fritzy before, but maybe I can modify it to act like a compass and lead us out of here."

"You can do that?"

"If it's not completely broken, yeah." Roxanne put the antenna on her knee while she started rooting around in her satchel. "And if the signal can get through the All-Mart's wall. And if he's still wearing the other one — they only work when they're plugged into meat."

"'*He* as in Mr. Hunter McRealMan?" Bernice sat up to watch as Roxanne found her tool box and took it out.

"Trig." Roxanne opened the tool box and grabbed a small needle-nosed probe. She poked at the exposed RATpack circuitry around the jack. "Or Trip. Something like that."

Bernice threw another napkin on the fire. "Wow, must have been real special."

"We had other priorities."

"So, this Trig guy, huge penis?" Bernice asked, running her finger luridly along the length of her cigarette holder.

Roxanne looked up from the antenna. "Little obsessed, aren't we?"

"So, Trig is tiny, then?"

"Trip. Pretty sure it was Trip. And what he had, he knew how to use." Roxanne gave the circuitry a final poke, blew on the jack, and *snick*ed it into the plug behind her ear. "There we go."

"Is it working?"

Roxanne frowned as she put the tool box back in her satchel. "It's powered up... but I'm not getting anything. Is it blinking?"

"You know how it was going all red before?"

"Yeah."

"It ain't doing that." Bernice tapped ashes into the burning, smoking pile of napkins. "It's back to yellow. Slow and steady."

"That's standby. So either it's working but can't get a signal, or it's still fritzing, or I broke it for good this time." Roxanne shrugged. "Well, it was worth a shot."

Bernice looked up. "Looks like Mother Superior's ready."

Roxanne got to her feet. "Total waste of time and effort."

"Hey, like you said, worth a shot, right?" Bernice asked, taking Roxanne's offered hand and pulling herself up. She stomped the fire out with the soul of a stiletto.

Mother Superior cleared her throat. "Gather into a line, girls."

The sisters did as instructed, standing shoulder to shoulder and all facing the same arbitrary direction Mother Superior was. They raised their arms to the All-Mart's ceiling as Mother Superior raised her medallion.

"Oh great anomaly of the Wasteland," Mother Superior began, "again we greet you!"

Her voice was swallowed up by the void stretching out in all directions.

"We hope — "

A noise behind them — a rhythmic hiss of clicking electrical discharges — interrupted her. Almost as one, the coven turned around towards the approaching sound.

"We have really got to stop praying to the damn thing," Roxanne whispered to Bernice.

"Hey," Bernice said around the cigarette holder, pointing its tip at Roxanne's ear. "The antenna, it's blinking red again."

"Seriously?" Roxanne's eyebrows crunched together as she reached for the antenna. "I don't feel anything... wait a sec. Maybe I do. It's kinda a tickle, like my leg's asleep, but the leg is way over there." She glanced over Bernice's shoulder. "I think somebody's on the line."

"How far away?"

Roxanne closed her eyes. "Not so far. Like, a couple miles. Inside the All-Mart, for sure."

"Somebody else with a RATpack antenna is in here?"

"These are paired. It'll only establish contact with the one other unit..." Roxanne's voice trailed off as the implications hit her and she broke into a grin. "Well, I'll be an incredibly hot niece of a monkey."

"He came in after you?" Bernice asked, exasperated. "I don't fuckin' believe this. I can't get a guy to give me the time of day, and you get them coming to rescue you after one roll in the hay."

Roxanne shrugged. "I think he had a friend. A lawyer, even."

"Look!" Georgina said, pointing out into the dark — which wasn't so dark anymore. "Lights!"

And they were coming their way.

Roxanne and Bernice turned and stared as row after row of ceiling arc lights began snapping to life with clanking electrical discharges. They came on in a wave that quickly passed over their heads, illuminating the vast, empty interior of the All-Mart, pock-marked only by thirty-foot high support beams at regular intervals.

"Whoa..." Bernice said.

"Yeah," Roxanne replied, her voice a reverent whisper.

Mother Superior beamed at the coven. "See, girls? The new god returns our welcome. Now maybe we can convince it to let us out." She turned her face back towards the ceiling, squinting into the harsh, bare white lights. "We hope you are pleased with the gifts we have provided, and that they have fed your mighty hunger, and now, satiated, you are prepared to forgive whatever transgression we have inadvertently and, I assure you, unintentionally —"

A hiss stopped her this time. A white noise hiss in the distance — from the same direction the lights had swept on. The hiss soon became a rumble, and as the coven watched, dozens upon dozens of columns of smoke erupted from the floor on the horizon and began creeping their way.

"What is that?" Bernice asked.

Roxanne's eyebrow went up. "I think they're... shelves?"

The lines of smoke grew nearer and nearer, leaving tall rows of rack shelving in their wake. As they grew closer, it became clear that the individual columns of smoke were clouds of nanochines, extruding the shelving from the store's floor in a buzzing, single-minded swarm.

Mother Superior lowered her arms and gestured for the coven to huddle around her. "Girls... tighten up, please."

The girls pressed in towards Mother Superior just as two columns of nanomachine swarms reached them, building shelves on either side of them.

"Okay." Roxanne watched one of the clouds building a shelf as it passed by. "This is both totally weirding me out but also maybe the coolest thing I've ever seen."

"You're very strange, Rox."

The nanomachine columns were soon past, and the girls were left staring at ten foot tall racks stretching back to the horizon, broken by regular gaps every hundred feet. The huddle loosened, the girls relieved. Curious, Roxanne took a step toward a rack and touched one of the empty shelves. It was warm. And getting warmer.

She withdrew her hand just as the shelf began to bubble.

Bernice peered over her shoulder. "What's it doing now?"

"I don't know."

"It's food!" Ophelia yelled. "It's making food!"

Roxanne and Bernice looked, and sure enough, a little further back down the shelf, All-Mart branded boxes of donuts and iced croissants were emerging from the bubbling shelf tops as if rising from underneath water. Further back, the shelves were already fully stocked with stacks of more boxes, bubbled up by nanochines from the shelves themselves.

"We were hungry, and the new god provided." Mother Superior bowed her head and raised her medallion to her lips, kissed it. "The new god is merciful," she said in a hushed, awe-filled voice.

Bernice reached for the nearest box of donuts as soon as it was done forming. Roxanne slapped the top of her hand.

"Oww!" Bernice exclaimed, reeling her hand back in. "What the fuck, Rox?"

"We're on a diet, remember?"

"But it's donuts..."

"We'll find something more hip-friendly." Roxanne frowned dubiously at the boxes, the donuts shiny and pristine under cellophane, almost as if they were made of wax. "Besides... something about nanomachine-produced food just doesn't sound right to me."

"Fine," Bernice pouted, crossing her arms over her chest.

"Well, I'm not on any diet." Xanadu slipped between Roxanne and Bernice to grab the box. "Pardon me." She flipped the box lid back, grabbed a donut — one with sprinkles — and started chowing down, the other girls watching to gauge her reaction, hunger in their eyes.

"How are they?" Bernice asked.

Xanadu swallowed the last bit, then shrugged. "A little stale —"

Xanadu's eyes suddenly went wide with panic. She dropped the box of donuts, her hands grabbing her stomach as she doubled over. Before anyone could step forward to help her, she had collapsed to the floor, writhing in pain.

"What's going on?" Mother Superior asked. "Is she choking?"

Roxanne crouched down in front of Xanadu. She had stopped writhing and was now curled up in a fetal position, her face buried in her hands. "Xan... are you okay?"

"I... don't... " Xanadu's hands parted and she looked up at Roxanne. A web-work of pulsing blue lines was spreading under her translucent skin from her lips and eyelids. Her eyes were blood-filled, swarming with tiny black dots. "I... don't... think... so..."

"The food!" Roxanne stood and rushed over to Georgina, slapping a croissant out of her hand just as the sixteen year old was about to bite into it.

Georgina glared at her. "What was that about?"

Roxanne said nothing in reply, only stepped aside and pointed down at an oddly grinning Xanadu, every inch of her skin now turning gray and fully covered in a fine web-work of pulsing blue.

Georgina screamed.

Roxanne looked at Mother Superior. "We can't eat this food. It's how they turn you into zombies."

Mother Superior nodded. "You hear that everyone? No food!" She crouched in front of Xanadu, reached out to stroke her hair, only to withdraw the hand as Xanadu hissed at her, a blood-black tongue darting out to lick blue lips.

"Umm... guys?" Bernice tapped Roxanne on the shoulder. "Not to pile it on, but we've got other problems." She thumbed down the aisle.

Roxanne twisted around to look. "Oh sweet mother of Jebus."

There, down the aisle a few hundred feet, was a frenzied mass of people making their halting, spastic way up the aisle. Dozens of them. Mostly adult men and women but a few snarling, screeching children. Their clothes were shreds, their skin translucent gray and mottled with pulsing blue webbing. They were pushing carts, biting and clawing at each other as they filled the carts by grabbing boxes at random from the shelves.

"What are they?" Bernice asked.

Her voice carried down the aisle. One of the things looked up, locking eyes with Bernice.

Roxanne was already reaching for Bernice's hand when the thing shrieked, prompting the others to stop their mindless shelf rifling and rush forward, clawed hands out-stretched and mouths slavering.

"Run!" Roxanne yelled, grabbing Bernice's hand and yanking her up the aisle. Stilettos clicking, they ran for the nearest gap, Roxanne tugging Bernie through it.

And right into the chest of a hulking, seven foot tall... thing. Maybe it was human once, but not anymore, not with that hard dark blue carapace skin and saucer-wide eyes glowing dull yellow. A security badge was set directly in the wrinkled flesh of its chest.

"Welcome to All-Mart," it said, its voice a deep growl. It reached a gnarled, almost crab-like hand around Roxanne's head to pluck the RATpack antenna out of her neck. "May I see your receipt?"

Chapter 10

TO THE RESCUE?

The *Wound* parked at the bottom of a hillock, Trip sat on the hood, leaned back against the windshield, smoking and staring all contemplative into the churning maelstrom of the All-Mart's looming expansion front only fifty feet away and growing closer, inch by slow inch.

"We don't even know if she's alive," Rudy said from under the car.

"All-Marts don't kill." Trip flicked the cigarette at the All-Mart with a sharp snap. It arced away and fell a little short, landing on his lap instead.

"You assume."

Trip sprung up and slid off the hood. The cig butt fell away and he batted at his jeans with both hands until he was sure he wasn't on fire. "Their original business model was to get market share. This one will have the same, meaning it just turns people into nanochine-filled zombie consumers."

"Bad enough," Rudy said between turns of a ratchet. "And begs the question, if we find her... how we gonna un-zombiefy her? Ask the nanochines to leave?"

"Yeah. Politely." Trip leaned against the fender, lit another cig. "Look, how the fuck do I know? We'll figure something out. You done under there yet?" he asked Rudy's hikers.

"Yeah. Give me a hand?"

Trip bent down, grabbed Rudy's ankles, and pulled. Once he was far enough out, Rudy sat up, slipping the ratchet into his bandolier and pulling a rag out of a thigh pocket. "We're all set." Rudy wiped his hands on the rag. "The anti-theft electric shock system will now, instead of delivering a semi-lethal shock of juice, give off a constant low-power, high-oscillation buzz-charge through the frame."

Trip had gone back to leaning against the fender. "Is that why my ass is tingling?"

Rudy stuffed the rag away and got to his feet. "I refuse to speculate about anything involving your ass."

"Wise choice."

"Anyway," Rudy said, leaning against the *Wound* next to Trip, "it should — maybe — discourage the All-Mart's nanochines from trying to break the car down into raw materials. Provided we don't stand still for long."

Trip smirked. "And the nanochines don't interpret the juice as a dinner bell."

"There is that." Rudy took out his calabash and held it between his teeth as he reached into the open passenger window to grab the tobacco can from the back seat. "But in that case, you'll have access to the off switch through your mind-machine interface."

"Won't be using it."

"Yeah, right." Rudy chuckled in disbelief, stuffing tobacco into the pipe with his thumb.

"I'm serious." Trip's hand sank into his jeans back pocket to pull out the RATpack antenna. He held it up to show Rudy. "I'll be jacked in to this instead."

"A WOLFpack antenna?" Rudy asked, throwing the can back into the car and lighting up.

"RATpack, actually. One of a pair." Trip blew on the jack plug then *snick*ed it into his socket. He felt it power on. "Roxanne has the other one. It should have pretty decent range. We get within twenty miles, we should get enough of a signal I should sense her, enough to get a general direction, anyway. Within a mile, we'll be able to communicate mind-to-mind. No memory sharing, though. That was pretty weird, so the firewall's staying up this time. Should still work."

"Well, you getting anything?"

"It might not be able to transmit/receive through that." Trip pointed the cigarette at the broiling dust and debris expansion front.

"Or," Rudy said, taking a long drag from the pipe and avoiding Trip's eyes, "those things only draw power when they're plugged in — and she's not plugged in."

Trip pushed himself off the fender and walked around the front of the *Wound*. "She'd better be wearing it, or she's pretty much screwed herself rescue-wise. The All-Mart's what, at least a hundred miles deep, ten wide? That's a lot of retail square footage to search just by driving around randomly."

"We could set up a grid pattern," Rudy suggested.

"I'll grid pattern you, you nerd. No, if she's half the babe I think she is, she'll know she should be wearing it."

"If she's not already a zombie."

Trip opened the driver's door. "Get in the car."

"Okay, ground rules." Trip settled in behind the steering wheel. The All-Mart looked even bigger and more menacing framed by the windshield. He forced himself to stop staring at it and smirk at Rudy. "There will be no mention of the irony here."

Rudy closed the passenger door as he got in. "But I came up with a whole list of one-line cheap shots. Some pretty good ones, too."

"And the first one you use will get you a karate-chop to the Adam's Apple."

Rudy grinned around his calabash. "Might be worth it."

"Second one, the karate-chop becomes a knife and the Adam's Apple your balls."

Rudy frowned. "You take the fun out of everything."

"That's what big brothers are for." Trip popped three caff pills from the Bugs Bunny dispenser onto his tongue. "You ready?"

"One sec." Rudy set the calabash in the open dash ashtray and reached into the back seat to grab a milk gallon of Morty's Finest and a spiked motorcycle helmet. He strapped the helmet down over his fez and stuck a bendy straw into the beer jug. He sucked up a good slug while rotating his left nipple all the way up. "Okay, now I'm ready."

Trip slipped the Pez dispenser away and sat back, lacing his fingers behind his head. "And we're off," Trip said, tensing for acceleration and twitching his left eyebrow.

Nothing happened.

Bewildered, Trip crunched his eyebrows at the steering wheel and twitched again. And again. And again, this time whacking his palm against the dash-mounted GameGear.

Rudy cleared his throat. "You're manual, remember?"

Trip grunted. "And you said I'd never need a second jack," He grabbed the steering wheel with one hand, shoved the *Wound* into Drive with the other, and stomped down hard on the gas. The *Wound* leapt forward, kicking up a cloud of dry wasteland behind it as launched towards the All-Mart.

"So," Rudy said, grabbing the dashboard, "pretty ironic, this."

"Right!" Charged by the caff pills hitting his system, Trip's hand left the steering wheel and flashed out like lightning into Rudy's throat, edge-on.

"Worth... it..." Rudy choked out, massaging his Adam's Apple as the *Wound* hit the expansion front.

Tendrils of nanochines struck out for the *Wound* as it sped through, only to snap back as if in pain, tendril tips sparking from contact with the car's electrically charged depleted uranium armor plating.

And then they were through. Into darkness that seemed to stretch out forever.

Trip twitched to turn on the hi-beams. When that didn't work, he swore, then pulled out the physical light knob. Twin beams stabbed out into the dark over endless bare concrete, illuminating row after row of support columns and empty space. He punched the scanner's activation sequence in to the GameGear — Up, Up, Down, Down, Left, Right, Left, Right, B, A — and after a moment the GameGear's tiny display screen blinked on, showing a wireframe representation of the All-Mart's interior.

Rudy released his death-grip on the dash and yawned. "That was fun." He took a sip from the beer jug and placed it on the seat next to him, then curled up against the passenger door. "Wake me up when we get there."

"Yeah, whatever." Trip slowed the *Wound* to around fifty miles per, slotting it between a row of support columns. He checked himself in the rear-view — the RATpack antenna was blinking yellow. He sighed. "Well, it was just an idea —"

He cut himself off as the antenna tip began blinking red, establishing a connection with its paired unit.

Roxanne's unit. Had to be.

Trip broke into a huge grin and jogged the steering wheel hard left, swinging the *Wound* to point towards the signal, and fishtailing the car's back end through a support column in the process.

Rudy grumbled, opening one eye briefly. "Hey, keep it down. Trying to nap here..."

———

Thirty seconds later. A mile deeper into the All-Mart. The ceiling lights were on now and the signal between the RATpack antennas was growing stronger every second.

Now was not the time for Rudy to be peacefully snoring away, Trip thought. He grabbed the jug of beer from the seat between them and poured it out over Rudy's crotch. Rudy came awake with a start, groggily looked down at his soaking lap. "What the...?"

Trip handed him the near empty jug. "You were drinking in your sleep."

"What, again?" Rudy sat up, draining the jug empty before noticing the blinking RATpack antenna. "That mean you're getting something?"

"Yeah. Decent signal, too."

"We close enough for contact?"

"Nah, we're still about three miles off, give or take. But it's got to be her, and she's making it easy on us. She's standing still."

Rudy nodded, stretched over the back of the front seat to grab another gallon of beer. Sorta-King Morty had stocked them well before sending them off on their mission. He uncapped it, took a swig. "You know, I was thinking... she didn't get snatched up by herself."

"Yeah, so?"

"We gonna try and help the others?"

"Hadn't really thought about it," Trip said, lighting a cig with the car lighter. He pushed the lighter back into the dash. "I suppose... no."

"Really?"

Trip shrugged. "I'm focused here. On Roxanne. Everybody else, let them find some other sucker to rescue them."

"Even the hot ones?"

"Well... okay, but they'd need to have rich dads willing to pony up a reward."

Rudy scowled. "How we supposed to figure out their parent's net worth? We gonna screen them?"

"It's not like we're gonna make them fill out a multi-page form, no. We'll just ask them to sign an affidavit." Trip took his eyes off the road just long enough to see

Rudy's confused expression. "What? You expect me to take their word for it?"

"I was thinking more along the lines of a chick for me, dude... doesn't necessarily have to be rich. Although it wouldn't —"

A shrill three-tone klaxon from somewhere in the dash interrupted him.

Trip yelled over the klaxon. "Okay, that's annoying! What is it?"

"The prox alarm," Rudy yelled back as he slapped his palms over his ears.

"Since when?"

"Since always!" Rudy yelled, thumbing the GameGear's D-Pad. The alarm went silent. "You just never hear it 'cause you're jacked in and the *Wound* filters it out for you."

"Well, it's awful."

"Supposed to be." Rudy pointed at the GameGear display. "Check it out."

Forgetting that the *Wound* was doing 120 miles per and needed his actual attention to keep going straight, Trip stared at the display and the blue dots popping up on it. Without the *Wound*'s interface, it took him a few moments to process what he was seeing — with the interface, he just would have felt the dots, known what they meant, no interpretation needed. "Yay, blips?" he asked as the *Wound* drifted to the right, sheering a support pole in half. It caromed through another and then another before Trip snapped his attention away from the screen and got her under control again.

"Vishnu's molars, I hate this," Trip growled, both hands in a white-knuckle death grip around the steering wheel. "How the fuck did people drive without interfaces? How the hell am I supposed to multitask? — But hey, we've got blips, right?"

"Yeah, blue blips." Rudy lowered the arms he'd thrown over his head while the *Wound* was getting pummeled by support columns.

"So?"

Rudy reached over the seat for the shotgun in the back seat. "The scanner's infrared. Blue blips mean zombies."

"You assume."

"It's a pretty solid assumption." Rudy cracked the shotgun open over his knees and shoved shells into it from his bandolier. "They're not warm, human bodies, that's for sure."

"Would they be that cold? I mean, they're not really undead. Just infected."

"The nanochines probably sink body temp way down to conserve energy."

"Wouldn't it be the other way around?" Trip stared out the windshield at row upon row of rack shelving that was seemingly growing out of the floor directly up ahead, like walls. He slammed on the brakes, took a hard right, and hit the gas, aiming the *Wound* between a pair of racks, barely a half foot of clearance on either side of the car. "Like, wouldn't they make their hosts run hotter, what with all that symbiotic energy leaching?"

"Do I look like a nano-engineer?" Rudy snapped the shotgun closed. "Wait a second... there's a red one. Two red ones... More. Lots more."

"Damn it."

"What? It's probably Roxanne and the Sisters. That's good news."

"Probably, yeah — expect I just lost the signal."

"Just now?"

"Yeah, gone, right when I'm about close enough to contact her mind-to-mind." Trip fingered the RATpack antenna. It was still firmly jacked in. "Like she disconnected."

Rudy's voice dropped. "Or got turned into a zombie."

"Shut up."

"Trip, all the reds are starting to turn blue."

"Okay, enough of this nonsense." Trip yanked the RAT-pack antenna out, tossed it up on the dash, and grabbed the *Wound*'s patch cord, *snick*ing it in to his skull. "There we are..." he said, smirking like a madman as the *Wound*'s familiar puppy-dog consciousness laid itself over his. And at the center of his joint consciousness, a half dozen red dots were slowly being surrounded by a whole bunch of blue ones.

A twitch of Trip's eyebrow and the *Wound* banked left, into and through a shelving rack, aiming straight for the cluster.

"A little warning next time," Rudy yelped, ducking low and throwing his arms over his head again.

"Oh, right," Trip said, as he had the *Wound* tear through another shelf. "Hold on!"

Chapter 11

MUFFINS AND ZOMBIES

The *Wound* spat out of an aisle stocked with breakfast muffins and into a cross aisle intersection filled with zombies and nuns. Trip twitched the brakes on just in time to avoid slamming through this old bare-breasted nun, her arms pinned behind her back by one zombie, another zombie trying to force-feed her a muffin. The *Wound* skidded to a stop, her front bumper stopping just inches short of the old nun's knees.

"Hey, I know those boobs..." Trip stared through the front windshield while the old nun fought futilely to keep muffin out of her mouth, alternately spitting and screaming, writhing in the zombie's grip. Both the zombies were wearing some kind of blue vest uniform, with name tags. Trip lit a cigarette.

"What are they doing?" Rudy's hand was under his t-shirt shirt, tweaking his nipple feverishly.

Trip unconsciously reached for the elephant revolver holstered on his thigh. Consciously, he twitched to lock the *Wound*'s doors. "I have no idea."

A third zombie in a blue vest stumbled up behind the old nun, took her head in his hands and held it rock-hard steady. The zombie holding her arms behind her back wrangled his free arm up to hold her mouth open. And that was that — the chesty old nun's mouth was soon stuffed to overflowing with muffin. The zombie feeding her held his hand over her mouth, forcing her to swallow. As soon as she did, all three zombies let her go and just shambled off.

"My conscious is telling me we should help." Rudy watched the old nun collapse, convulsing, in front of the *Wound*. "But my gut is telling me we should run away, very fast —"

Rudy cut himself off with a yelp as the old nun sprung up, her skin a patchwork of spiderweb-like softly glowing blue lines, her eyes glazed. Hunched, she glared at them through the windshield, her now dark azure tongue licking mottled lips. Rudy sunk low in his seat, his head dipping below the dash. Trip pulled the revolver from its holster, leveled it square between her eyes, and cocked it.

The zombie nun stared down the barrel. After a second's standoff, she let out a quiet, snorting laugh, then shrugged, spinning around on one stiletto heel and shambling off towards a shelf of iced toaster cakes where another nun-turned-zombie — a cute black chick with exceptionally long legs and ripped fishnets — was tearing into boxes and ravenously stuffing cakes into her mouth two at a time.

Trip smirked and holstered the revolver. "Shatner knows I've never agreed with your conscious, and I don't actually think there's anything we <u>can</u> do for them... but we can't run away just yet." He looked around the intersection, both with his own eyes and the *Wound*'s sensors. "You see Roxanne?"

Rudy craned his neck to peer out over the dash. "I don't think so." He sunk back down, grabbing the shotgun from the dash as he did and hugging it tight to his chest.

All around the intersection, nuns turned zombies were rifling the shelves, tearing into food. Trip did a quick head-count. Nine nuns. All zombies. The blue-vested zombies with the name tags were long gone. "Me either."

"Maybe they didn't get her," Rudy said, his optimism betrayed by his voice breaking. "Or she got separated..."

Trip sat back, closed his eyes, and focused on what the *Wound*'s sensors were showing him. "There's a red blip a couple rows over and running. Might be her. She's got a couple blue blips on her ass. Grab something." He twitched the *Wound*'s brakes off and hit the gas, sending the *Wound* barreling down an aisle, just missing a nun-zombie tearing into a bag of All-Mart branded cheese-curls.

Bernice was half-running, half-hopping down an aisle of baby toys. Ten or so strides back she'd lost a stiletto heel, which wasn't making it any easier to stay ahead of the pair of snarling, slobbering zombie things in blue vests lopping after her.

Run faster! Bernice's id yelled at her between gasps for air.

Her ego panted back: *You know running's not my thing. Now sleeping, that I could do faster...*

Run faster damn it!

You run faster, I'm about dead here.

For the love of the gods, shut up and just run!

Or I could give up.

How about running faster?

How bad can being a zombie be?

Bad.   Very   bad. That-time-when-we-were-nine-and-Uncle-Stanis-law-put-his-hand-on-our-inner-thigh bad.

Okay, sure, the chances of us ever getting laid might go way, way down, but there'd be food — lots of food.

Seriously, just run!

The left side of her stomach cramped up, her pace slowed. *I'm so tired, and they have donuts...* her ego sighed.

Okay, okay, how about we make a deal? her id suggested in a panic while she pressed down hard on her stomach with the flat of her hand.

What kind of deal?

You keep running and when we get out of this, diet's off.

Oh no it's not, her super-ego chimed in from the depths.

Quiet, you, her id and ego shot back simultaneously.

Don't listen to her, her id continued. *We'll make it happen. No diet.*

Yes, her super ego said, *because we all know men really dig fat chicks. The fatter the better. Uncle Stan loves 'em fat.*

Is now really the time to be having this discussion? her id asked.

We can't get a man now, her super ego went on, *and you're ten pounds shy of Rubenesque, so let's put on more weight... yes, that makes sense.*

Rubenesque? Her ego protested. *More like Amazonian ...*

Her super ego snorted. *About a foot and a half shy for that, dear...*

Will you two shut up? her id pleaded. *They're getting closer!*

"Closer?" Bernice whispered aloud, glancing behind her. The zombies were right there, on her heels, arms outstretched, gnarled fingertips reaching for her, inches from her shoulder.

She screamed.

And then they were gone.

Swept up and slammed away as something big and brown and fast and armored-plated came skidding sideways through the shelving on her right. Reflexively she crouched, throwing her arms over her face, peeking out to watch as the car kept sliding, slamming the zombies into the opposite rack of shelves and pining them between the shelves and the passenger side before finally coming to a stop.

Bernice lowered her arms and slowly stood up, stared at the zombies, their bodies crushed and all jangled up with the mangled shelving. After a good long second Bernice realized she was still alive and remembered to breath.

Then this tall, kind of horse-faced guy wearing a long-tailed tux jacket and black jeans was getting out of the car, pulling a comically oversized revolver and raising it over the open car door, pointing it at her.

All she could do was stare down the huge barrel, eyes wide, like a deer caught in headlights.

"Down!" the guy shouted, cocking the gun. "Now!"

She dropped like a stone, squeezing her eyes shut and pressing herself flat against the concrete just as the guy fired over her.

BOOM!

The retort was deafening. Blanked out all other sound with this high-pitched whine.

Bernice opened her eyes, looked back at what the guy had shot at. Another zombie, his blue apron splattered with his own blue-gray blood from the jagged hole punched through his right shoulder. His arm was just dangling there loose by a few ligaments, but the zombie was still running, still heading towards her.

BOOM!

The shot tore into the zombie's abdomen, ripped it open, taking a good portion of intestines, stomach and kidney with it as it punched out through the zombie's back.

But the thing still kept on running. Faster, now.

The zombie let out an angry yell that pierced through the white-noise whine of the gunshots, and leapt. Right over Bernice and straight for tall guy.

BOOM!

And just like that, the zombie had a hole the size of a bowling ball through his chest and Bernice was being showered in bits of blue-gray lung and bone.

The zombie went limp in mid-air. Tall Guy stepped to the side — putting the revolver barrel's tip to his lips and blowing away the smoke — just as the zombie hit the floor in a crumpled mess where he'd been standing. Tall Guy smirked, poked the toe of his red high-tops into the zombie's side.

"Hey, lookie there, it's dead," Tall Guy said, smiling at himself. "Yay, me."

"Yeah, well," said a second guy, getting out of the driver's side, "I would'a had him if you hadn't pinned my door shut." He was short, muscular, cute — especially the darling little red soul patch — and carrying a sawed-off shotgun. He walked around the front of the car to stand next to Tall Guy and stared down at the zombie.

"Did you a favor." Tall Guy holstered the big revolver. "If you'd tried to down him with that pea-shooter of yours, you'd be picking zombie teeth out of your neck right now."

"Bullshit!" Soul-patch touched his bandolier. "These shells are packed with high-density micro-explosives. They would have vaporized his head into a cloud of fine red mist."

"Sure, once he got within range." Tall Guy lit a cigarette. "Which is what? About zombie-arm length, right? Like two feet?"

"Three," Soul-patch said, frowning. "Okay, two-and-a-half."

Bernice sat up, cleared her throat. "Never mind the damsel in distress here."

Tall Guy glanced at her and smirked. "You're welcome."

"Oh, sorry, yeah," Soul-patch said, slipping the shotgun into a harness on his back and walking over to her. He extended a hand down to her and grinned optimistically. "You okay?"

"That depends." Bernice took his hand. Firm and strong. She let him pull her up. He didn't strain at all. "You gonna get me out of here?"

"Your parents got money?" Tall Guy asked as he strode up next to Soul-patch.

"What?" Bernice asked.

"Ignore him," Soul-patch said. "We can get you out of here."

Tall Guy rolled his eyes and walked off to examine the zombies the car had pinned to the racks.

Bernice checked herself out. Nothing broken or missing. Just a lot of blue-gray zombie blood splatter. "Then, yeah, I'm okay." When she looked up, she noticed Soul patch's camos were wet in the crotch. "What's with the... you have a little accident?"

He blushed. "Oh. No. Spilled some beer."

"Beer? You got any left?"

He smiled. Dopey, but cute. "Whole backseat."

Bernice returned the smile. Normally, that'd be the whole of it — she'd clam up and look away, embarrassment over actually talking to a guy catching up to her. But not this time. Roxanne's advice to be aggressive rang in her ears — and given extra urgency by the absolutely shitty day she'd been having. "My kind of guy."

His smile got a lot bigger and dopier. "Really?"

Bernice grabbed his head between her hands and pulled his surprised face towards hers, planting a long, deep kiss on him.

After a moment, she let him go. He just stared at her, wide-eyed.

"For rescuing me," she said. A pause, then, "Too much?"

His wide-eyed stare broke into a panicked head-shaking. "No... no, not at all..."

"All right, there'll be plenty of time for you two to get acquainted in the back seat later," Tall Guy said, returning. He pointed his cigarette up and down Bernice's body. "I'm assuming by the getup, you're a Sister of No Mercy, so I'm betting you know who Roxanne is."

"Roxanne... sure, she's — Oh, shit!" Bernice exclaimed. "You're the guy! You're Mr. Hunter McRealMan."

Tall Guy's face went confused. "Huh? Who?"

"Trig, right?" Bernice asked.

"Trip."

"And I'm Rudy," Soul-patch said.

"Hey, Rudy," she said, giving him a hungry smile. He blushed. She was beginning to enjoy this aggressive thing. She offered her hand out to him. "Bernice. Bernie. You can call me Bernie."

Rudy took her hand and giggled sheepishly. "Hi." He didn't shake it, but he wasn't letting it go, either.

"Concentrate." Trip took both their wrists and pulled their hands apart. "Where's Roxanne?" he asked her.

"I dunno. We were running from shoppers, and this big brute with a badge pops up in front of us. It grabbed Rox — just took her, dragged her off, and left me there. I doubled back to join the others but by then all these other zombies had showed up and were force-feeding everyone, and that's when I took off again." She gave Rudy a devilish little smile, taking a step closer to him, puffing up her cleavage. "Thanks again for the save."

Rudy swallowed, struggled to not stare. "I was just... I..."

Trip sighed. "I'm the one who did the actual saving, let's not forget."

"That's nice," Bernice said, running her finger down Rudy's bandolier. "So, you mentioned beer?"

"Ummm...yeah..." Rudy watched her fingertip slowly work its way down towards his belly. "Coming right up." He reluctantly backed away, all the way back to the car, nervously waving at her while he did.

"You say they *took* Roxanne?" Trip stepped in front of her. "Why'd they take her instead of force-feeding her like the others?"

"You're asking me?" Bernice reached into her purse and took out something wrapped in tissue paper. She handed it to Trip. "But might have something to do with this."

Trip unwrapped it. "Her RATpack antenna?"

Bernice nodded. "Yeah. The fucker took it off her and dropped it when he dragged her off."

"That must have been when you lost contact," Rudy said, returning with a milk jug of beer. He held it out to Bernice.

Bernice took the jug with a smile, uncapped it, and drank. "She thought you were jacked in and near, that second time." She handed the jug back to Rudy.

"There was a first time?" Trip asked.

"Just before the All-Mart snatched us up, during the appeasement ceremony. The antenna looked like it was connected — it went all blinky red — but she wasn't feeling anybody on the other end. You weren't sneaking a peek at the ceremony, were you?"

"The thought had occurred to me," Trip said with a half-smile. "But no. We were still in Shunk. Pressing business."

"That's what we figured. She thought it was on the fritz."

"Weird." Trip stuffed the antenna away in a tux pocket. "But irrelevant. Any idea where they took Roxanne?"

She shook her head. "I just got here myself."

Rudy stopped staring longingly at her over the beer jug long enough to ask, "Do you remember what direction it dragged her off in?"

She pointed off into the distance. "Maybe that way."

"Maybe?" Trip asked.

She scowled at him. "I was a little stressed at the time."

"It's okay," Rudy said.

"No, no it's not okay," Trip said. "We don't even have a signal to follow anymore. Who knows where —"

A low, growling moan interrupted him. All three turned to look. It was coming from the zombie had Trip shot.

"You put three rounds through it — how is it not dead?" Rudy asked.

Trip drew his revolver and cautiously stepped up closer to the zombie. The hole in his chest was closing, the skin resealing itself over undulating, re-growing lungs and heart. The other two wounds were already gone.

"Great. Self-healing zombies. Fucking nanochines." Trip flicked his cigarette into the zombie's chest cavity just as it sealed itself shut. Trip cocked the revolver and pointed it at the zombie's forehead. "Let's see if the oldie-but-goodie bullet through the brain does the trick."

"Wait," Rudy said. "Don't kill it."

"Why the fuck not?"

"Karma."

"Fuck Karma."

"Other way around if you keep pissing it off, bro." Rudy pointed at the two zombies pinned to a rack by the *Wound*, writhing and struggling to free themselves but not having any luck. They were good and stuck, and helpless. "Look, they're not a threat to us. Let's just leave them here and get going."

"Going where?" Trip waved the revolver randomly above his head. "'Maybe that way' isn't a real direction."

"Killing zombies isn't going to help."

"Oh, it'd help," Trip grunted, holstering the revolver.

Rudy smiled, looked down at the zombie at Trip's feet. The zombie's wounds had almost completely healed and it was just starting to come awake. "Anyway... I've got an idea about how we might figure out where to go."

Chapter 12

BOB

"Welcome to All-Mart. How can we change your life today?"

According to the nametag half-grown into his chest, the zombie's name was Bob. He hung spread-eagled on a rack of green polka-dotted teddy bears, electric extension cords lashed tight around his wrists, ankles, waist and throat. Neither his body nor his uniform showed any signs he'd been shot by Trip, the wounds healed and the fabric regrown by the All-Mart nanochines in his blood and living in the fabric of his clothes.

"This was your whole idea?" Trip was up on the *Wound*'s hood, leaned back on the windshield. He looked up from re-reading the Steve Martin Playboy interview. "Strap the zombie up to a rack and stare at him until he says something other than 'Welcome to All-Mart, how can we change your life today'?"

"I really think it's starting to get to him." Rudy was standing in front of Bob, staring up at the zombie as he thoughtfully puffed on his calabash. "Just give it some time."

Trip set the Playboy down next to him and slid off the hood. He stepped up next to Rudy. "You've already been at it for ten minutes."

Rudy frowned at him. "You're not exactly one to talk about taking your time, Mr. 'I-haven't-met-a-lock-I-can't-crack'."

Bernice was standing off to the side, arms crossed over her chest. "I don't get it. He's a zombie. Just torture him."

Trip smirked. "Oh, no, we couldn't do that."

"Why not?"

Growling, Trip pointed at Rudy.

Rudy smiled at Bernice. "Karma."

"Karma?"

Rudy nodded. "The more you hurt others for no reason, the more you get hurt back."

"Yeah, I know what it is, but... it did attack me." Bernice jogged her head back at the two zombies still pinned between the *Wound* and the rack it had crashed into. Their wounds had healed but they were trapped pretty good, despite their continuing, writhing efforts to free themselves. "All three of them did."

Rudy puffed at his calabash. "And we roughed 'em up good. But the threat's over. Always defense, never attack. Read that at an amusement church, once. It's good advice. Keeps the soul clean."

Bernice sighed. "So we're just gonna stand here and ask nicely?"

"You'll see — he'll come around once he sees we're being all civil." Rudy looked up at Bob. "We might even offer him some lunch later, if he cooperates."

Bernice turned to Trip. "You believe this?"

"Believe it? I've had to put up with it my whole life. But not today." Trip pulled his elephant revolver from his holster. "No time for this shit."

Rudy stepped in front of him. "Dude. Karma."

"You're trying to appeal to a zombie's civil side." Trip's thumb rubbed against the revolver's hammer, itching to pull it back. "Zombies don't have civil sides."

"There's still a person in there."

"Under about a million body- and mind-controlling nanochines that we have to get through first. I don't see how we're gonna do that without some good old-fashioned Rumsfielding." Trip leaned close to Rudy, lowered his voice. "Besides, I think you're losing Cleavage here."

Rudy stole a glance over at Bernice. She was glaring up at Bob, rubbing her fist with her palm. "You think?"

Trip nodded. "She seems like the aggressive kind... you know, into real men. Not pussies."

"Fine." Rudy gestured for Trip to put his gun away. "But I'll do it. Your karma debt's big enough as it is, no need to risk tipping it over and having an asteroid fall on you or something. Especially when I'm standing next to you."

Trip smiled. "Just get him talking."

Rudy patted the ashes from his pipe and jammed it into his bandolier. "Right. Right. Okay, give me some room. Okay, how we wanna do this?" Rudy asked himself as Trip and Bernice took a few steps back. Rudy cracked his knuckles and, chewing his lower lip, surveyed the rack of baby toys next to Bob. After a good long moment, Rudy grabbed a yellow rubber duck from a bin. He turned back towards Bernice. "You might want to, you know, avert your eyes, this could get nasty."

She stared at the duck dubiously. "I don't see how."

"Sorry about this..." Rudy said to Bob as he wrapped his hand around the rubber duck and punched the zombie in the gut.

The rubber duck squeaked.

Bob, he didn't even notice he'd been hit.

"Huh," Rudy said, staring at the rubber duck in his hand, "that should'a worked."

Trip bowed his head and pinched the bridge of his nose between his index finger and thumb. "Oh, for Shatner's sake."

"Mind if I give it a try?" Bernice asked, taking the rubber duck from Rudy. "I've got a badge in discipline."

Rudy's eyes went wide and he swallowed. "You've got a badge in discipline?"

"Since I was thirteen," she said proudly, tossing the rubber duck away over her shoulder. "Second badge I earned after indoor horticulture." She turned to Trip. "Well?"

Trip stepped aside and swept his hand towards the zombie. "Be my guest."

She pointed at his revolver. "May I?"

Trip thought for a moment, then shrugged, taking it out and handing it to her handle-first. "Be gentle with her."

Bernice nodded, brushed hair from her face, and strode up to the spread-eagled zombie, cocking the revolver. While Bob looked down at her, his blue-bloodshot eyes trembling, she raised the gun.

"Welcome to All-Mart..." he said. Then she fired, the revolver's barrel pushed hard into the flesh of Bob's left thigh, tearing a hole in it the size of a baseball, exposing bone. Bob howled, writhed in pain. Somehow, through the howling, he managed to stutter out: "How... can... we... change your world today?"

"Now that's how you interrogate a zombie." Trip smirked back at Rudy then stepped up behind Bernice. He pointed at Bob's face. The blue-gray spiderwebbing had, if only momentarily, narrowed and dimmed, and had even slightly retracted around Bob's lips and eyes. "See that?"

Rudy pursed his lips in distaste, and nodded. "Yeah. The pain must make the nanochines recede temporarily. Probably being diverted to repair the damage from the impact." The hole in Bob's leg began knitting itself closed and the blue-gray spiderwebbing of his skin regained its regular thickness and glow.

"Keep going," Trip encouraged Bernice.

Bob's eyes followed the barrel as Bernice shifted it from his left to his right thigh. He writhed harder, trying to escape the inevitable —

BOOM!

"Welcome to All-Mart!" Zombie Bob howled out at first, then as his skin cleared — becoming almost line free — he snapped his head down towards Bernice. "Will you please stop that?"

"Now we're getting somewhere." Trip nudged Bernice aside. "So, Bob... where'd they take Roxanne?"

"Who? What are you talking about?" Zombie Bob asked just as the spiderwebbing spread out across his face once again. "...How can we change your world today?"

Trip rolled his eyes. "Bernice, if you please? Something a little harder to heal this time."

Bernice nodded and casually shot Bob's kneecap off.

After the screaming died down and his skin cleared, Bob choked out: "Okay, okay... what was the question?"

Trip smiled up at him, holding his hand at shoulder height. "Friend of ours. About this tall. Black hair. Great ass. Guy with a badge dragged her off."

"Security," Bob said, his voice strained from the pain of his kneecap being rebuilt. "Sounds like security."

"Okay, *security* dragged her off." Trip took the cigarette from his mouth and pointed with it. "In that general direction. What's that way?"

"Housewares," Bob said after thinking a moment. "Then sporting goods. Ladies undergarments is a few miles beyond that."

"Maybe they just want her to model some bras," Rudy suggested.

Bernice shook her head. "If that's what they wanted someone for, let's be honest, they picked the wrong gal."

"Yes, yes, we all know about your impressively big rack, but can you please put it away before Rudy has an aneurism?" Trip asked her, then turned back to question Bob. "That all that's in that direction, Bob?"

"No," Bob said. The blue spiderwebbing glow reappeared around his eyes and mouth, spreading out slowly over his face, and he struggled to speak. "There's more store. Associate settlements... Then much more store... And... eventually... Origin."

"What's Origin?" Trip asked, jogging his head at Bernice. She nodded back with a smile, jammed the barrel of the revolver into Bob's re-growing kneecap. It sunk deep into the still soft bone as she twisted it, shoved it on through.

"Origin!" Bob screamed from the pain. The spiderwebbing dimmed and retracted. Bob panted, waiting to speak until Bernice had pulled the revolver away and stepped back. "The heart of All-Mart. Where it began... where it spreads out from. Home."

"That's got to be where they took her." Bernice wiped Bob's blood and bone tissue from the revolver's barrel on her miniskirt.

"That where they took her, Bob?" Trip asked.

"I don't know... cannot say..." Glowing spiderwebbing reappeared over Bob's entire face. "How can we change your life today?"

Trip grabbed his revolver back from Bernice and jammed the barrel into Bob's ruined knee.

Bob screamed, breaking into tears of pain as the spiderwebbing fully retracted again. "Please... please... stop doing that!"

Trip smirked at him. "Give us a straight answer."

"All right, all right," Bob said. "The Voice. It told Security to find her and bring her to Origin."

"What 'voice'?" Trip asked.

"The Voice!" Bob lifted his head, smiling warmly at the ceiling. "The pretty Voice. The powerful Voice."

Trip sighed. "Let me guess... this voice, it comes from Origin?"

"It is Origin."

"Great. So Origin's a voice..."

Bob's smile widened. "And a city, a great city only the most trusted Associates and Security are honored to inhabit."

"A zombie city. Terrific." Rudy tweaked his nipple before wandering off down the aisle muttering to himself. "Should have blown my own brains out when I had the chance."

"Heavily defended, I take it?" Trip asked Bob.

Bob nodded. "Security keeps a high profile, yes."

"Well, then, no shoplifting, kids. All right, let's get going to this Origin place, see if we can find Roxanne." Trip spun around to see Rudy spooning two fingers worth of All-Mart branded Enriched Applesauce baby food into his mouth.

Rudy looked up at Trip and Bernice staring at him, dumfounded alarm on their faces. "What?" Rudy licked his fingers. "You were serious about not shop-lifting?"

Trip scowled. "Did you not see what happens when you eat the food here?"

Rudy's face went dire. "Fuck... oh, well. Damage done." He shrugged, scooped another couple fingers worth into his mouth. He swallowed, raised his eyebrows at their blank stares. He licked his fingers clean. "What? My chem factory should be able to fight off the nanochines."

"You'd better hope they can," Trip said.

Bernice stepped up to Rudy and, smiling sadly, took the baby food from him. She put the half empty jar on a shelf and stared at him, her brow crinkled with concern.

"Seriously, I'll be okay." Rudy pulled up his t-shirt and rubbed his hairy stomach. "Iron belly."

Bernice pulled his t-shirt down. "Just no more snacks, okay?" she asked, taking his hand and leading him to the *Wound*.

As they walked by him, Trip took a final drag off his cig and flicked it away, then started back to the *Wound* himself.

"Hey, wait, what about me?" Bob asked.

Trip didn't stop. "What about you?" he asked over his shoulder.

"At least let me down."

"So you can go warn your zombie pals and that Voice thingee?"

"The Voice already knows," Bob said, jogging his head at the two zombies pinned between the *Wound* and a shelf rack. They'd given up writhing and were now simply watching Rudy hold the door open so Bernice could crawl into the back seat of the *Wound*.

Trip stopped at the *Wound*'s bumper and spun around. "You know the way to Origin?"

Bob nodded his head. "Yeah."

Trip smiled.

Chapter 13

BACKSEAT EXPOSITION

Rudy leaned forward, checked himself in the *Wound*'s rear-view. He ran his fingers over his cheek and chin. "Am I getting... glow-y?"

Trip twitched to turn on the ceiling light and glanced over. He didn't see any blue-glowing spiderwebbing, and he hadn't the other dozen times in the last two hours Rudy had asked. "Your skin does have a certain pallid sheen to it... although that might just be fear and loathing." Outside, endless shelves of camping gear flashed by at fifty-miles-per with maybe two inches clearance on either side. The steering wheel jiggled back and forth on its own, the *Wound* making constant micro-adjustments while Trip chain-smoked and played Tetris on a first-gen GameBoy Rudy had converted to draw power from contact with skin. "But maybe I should just put one in your brain now as a precaution."

Rudy slumped back. "That's a little extreme, don't you think?" His hand slipped under his t-shirt to turn his nipple up all the way.

"And hilarious." Trip returned his attention to the game. "Plus, it's win-win, either way."

Rudy's brow crunched. "How you figure that?"

"If it doesn't heal, we know you're not a zombie, and my trust in you will be restored — I'll even say as much during your eulogy. But if it does heal itself, sure, you're a zombie, but you might come out better for the deal. Maybe the nanochines can fix the damage from that time you got dropped on your head when you were six months old."

"Oh, you mean the time you dropped me on the head when I was six months old?"

"Yes, okay, that time." Trip winced as an L-block landed the wrong way up, cutting off a Tetris he'd been constructing. "But don't go blaming that on me. Blame mom. Who gives an 18-month old an infant to hold, anyway?"

"She needed her hands free — we were kinda in a firefight at the time."

"So it's no surprise I dropped you."

"More like threw me at the bad guys."

"Only as a diversionary tactic to save myself. And that's another thing... who takes her kids on a hit?"

"She couldn't find a sitter. Again, all your fault."

"Sure, bite one sitter's tit and you're blackballed for life." Trip tossed the GameBoy onto the dash. "You didn't see me raising a stink about her boobs being dry wells, did you?"

Rudy crossed his arms over his chest. "She was in her sixties."

"Still had a nice rack, though." Trip grabbed the rear-view, re-adjusted it to point into the back seat. Bob the Zombie and Bernice were sitting as far apart as they could, eyeing each other suspiciously over the pile of beer jugs stacked up between them. Bob was tightly bound in loops extension cord, his arms immobile. "So, Bob, what can Rudy expect in his new life as a zombie?"

"Knock it off, will ya?" Rudy sunk further down into his seat, crossing his arms over his chest and sulking.

"Knowing is half the battle," Trip said back, nodding at Bob to answer the question.

Bob shrugged, kept his eyes on Bernice. "Well, it's actually not all the bad... when people aren't shooting or stunning or hitting you."

"Which reminds me..." Trip balled his right hand into a fist and shot it out at Rudy's left temple.

Rudy screamed. "What the fuck was that for?"

Trip chuckled. "Just trying to keep you human, bro."

"Asshole," Rudy snarled out, rubbing his temple with the palm of his hand. "You don't get to hit me. Anybody's doing anything to me, it's Bernice."

Trip shook his head. "Oh, no, you'd both enjoy that way too much. — But that does remind me... Bernice?"

Bernice smiled, reached over the beer jug pile and shoved the snapping and sparking business end of Rudy's shock baton into Bob's shoulder, holding it there for a count of three before withdrawing it with a full-toothed smile. Bob went into convulsive spasm, the faint trace of glowing spiderwebbing around his eyes retreating. "Damn it," he said after catching his breath, "you have to lay it on so hard?"

"Stop being such a baby," Bernice told him. She laid the baton on her lap, opened a fresh milk jug of beer. "Okay, here's a question for you, zombie. Where'd the All-Mart come from?"

"What do you mean?" Bob asked warily.

Bernice took a slug then handed the jug over the front seat to an appreciative Rudy. "The Tome of Speculation says the All-Marts were corporate weapons used to aggressively capture market share in Central America, way back in Megacorp War II: The Revengening. But that war ended forty years ago, and long before that all the All-Marts had been neutralized and torn down. But then this one just pops up out of nowhere ten years back — and a couple thousand miles north of Central America — and starts spreading out over the wasteland. Why? The Tome doesn't even speculate."

"Give the zombie a break, Cleavage." Trip smirked at Bernice through the rear-view. "He's had a rough day. Bad enough we have to shock him every ten minutes —"

"More like five," Bob noted.

"— whatever." Trip snorted. "I'm just saying, he probably doesn't appreciate all the questions."

"It's okay," Bob said. "It's nice just talking, again. We mostly communicate non-verbally. But truth is, I don't know."

"What does it matter?" Trip lit a cigarette. Not that many left in the tin, he noted with a sour frown. "It's here, it's not bothering anybody."

"Except the people it turns into zombies," Bernice said.

Bob shook his head. "Not bothering us, either. It's saving us. Before I walked in, I had nothing —"

"Wait a second." Rudy wiped beer from his lips with the back of his hand and handed the jug back to Bernice. "You walked in? Voluntarily?"

"Yeah. And it was the best decision we ever made."

"We?" Rudy asked.

Bob looked out the window at the shelves flashing by. "There were about two dozen of us at the end — all that was left after our town got taken over by a WOLFpack. We'd been doing the nomad thing for a while, but it was hard. Real hard. The things we did for food and shelter... I don't like remembering. And that was when we could find either. We never knew when one of us might go missing in the middle of the night — kidnapped by raiders or dragged off by an animal. But then we came across the All-Mart. We'd heard the stories about being turned into zombies, but at that point, we were desperate. We figured it was better being a zombie than what we were."

Bernice took a slug of beer. "I'd rather be dead in the wasteland than a zombie in here."

Bob turned away from the window towards her. "You say that, but you don't know. I mean, my old life, it seems unreal, and right now, I feel okay — but unnatural. Like I'm dreaming — more like I'm having a nightmare. I can't wait to wake up and be myself again."

Bernice smirked. "My friends didn't ask to be zombies. They aren't better off."

"I'm just speaking for myself," Bob said. "I'm part of something. I've got a job, a reason to exist. Plus, I eat regular. And I'm safe. My family's safe. Hell, if it wasn't for the All-Mart, I wouldn't have met my wife."

"You met her in here?" Rudy asked.

"Yeah, of course. She's security. She was working Tween board games, same as I was, and we hit it off just about instantly over a game of 'Sparkly Mystery Dude.' Nine months later, we had Ty."

"A zombie baby?" Trip asked.

Bob smiled proudly. "He's gonna be an associate, just like his dad. His little sister, Denise, we won't know for another year when the specialization kicks in, but her mom's already hoping for security. Made her a little badge and everything."

"Weird." Bernice took another sip of beer.

"What's so weird about it?" Bob asked. "We have lives here. Good lives. We don't get sick. We live practically forever... and the All-Mart provides everything we need."

"See, there you go." Trip raised an eyebrow at Bernice through the rear view. "However this thing ended up being here — let's just say it sprang up spontaneously from the desert — it's a good thing. And if any one individual played a minor and quite accidental part in it, they should probably get a medal or something."

Bernice scowled at him. "Or a good punch in the temple. With brass knuckles. Or one of those spikey things."

Rudy shot Trip a sideways glance, and Trip cleared his throat, tapped on the GameGear display. The wireframe showed miles of shelves around them, with a few dozen blue dots scattered around. "Anybody else thinkin' it's odd we haven't seen any security? Zombie — you weren't kidding about the Voice knowing we're here, right?"

"The Voice knows everything," Bob said. "Because we tell her everything."

Trip twisted around, put his arm up on the back of the front seat, and smirked at Bob. "So why hasn't it sent somebody to convert us? Or fetch us like it did Roxanne?
"

"In all my time here, the Voice has never asked that anyone be brought to it before today. Your friend must be special."

"Special how?"

"The Voice didn't say. Only that it wanted her."

"And it didn't want us?" Rudy asked.

Bob shook his head at Rudy. "It didn't say anything about you — but that's normally how it works. The Voice doesn't get involved. Us associates are programmed to convert any people we come across by force-feeding. But since the All-Mart is so big, and there's only a few thousand associates, the food's all laced with conversion nanochines, too. So, even if by chance somebody doesn't run across one of us, they're going to eat eventually, and join us. Everyone just sorta joins us, one way or another, and the Voice doesn't have to intervene." His face darkened. Not with blue spider-webbing but with remembered dread. "If the shoppers don't get them first, that is."

"'Get them'?" Trip asked.

"Shoppers are... you just want to avoid them, okay? Every day I thank the Voice I was converted into an Associate and not a Shopper. They're ravenous. Like animals. They're programmed to consume, and that's about it. They'll go into an area and pick the shelves clean — and then when they are, they'll then turn on each other or anybody else around, non-converted and Associates, even their fellow shoppers, doesn't matter, until the shelves are restocked. Unless Security's around. They won't mess with security."

"So, anywhere there are a couple thousand of them just standing around, we shouldn't go anyway near, then, I take it?" Trip asked.

"Definitely," Bob said. "Even Security runs the other way when there are more than a few dozen in one place."

"Man," Trip said, twisting back around to gesture out the windshield. "I wish you'd told me that about thirty seconds ago."

Chapter 14

LADIES WEAR

The *Wound* shot out of Sporting Goods into a forest of mushroom-shaped clothes racks freshly stocked with women's casual business attire. Thousands of shopper zombies — clothed in rags and slobbering — jockeyed for position around the racks, grabbing anything they could reach, tearing and ripping at their fellow shoppers just to get at the cheap gray pantsuits.

"Dear Shatner..." Not taking his eyes off the scene out the windshield, Rudy swallowed and reached for the double-barrel sawed-off on the dash. "It's like a piranha feeding frenzy."

"They're... horrible." Bernice turned to look at Bob over the pile of beer jugs. "Is that what happened to the Mother Superior and the others? Are they shoppers now?"

"It's all based on the population of the All-Mart when you're converted — what you become depends on what the All-Mart needs to keep the population in proportion. Two percent of the population needs to be security. Eight, associates. Ninety percent, shoppers."

"Ninety percent?" Bernice's shoulders drooped. "Then they're probably..."

"Yeah," Bob said. "Odds are. But they won't be shoppers, yet. Everybody starts out as a wanderer."

"A wanderer?" Rudy asked, cracking open the shotgun to make sure it had fresh shells.

Bob nodded. "The All-Mart's nanochines need a good day or two to really integrate with their host. So while they're working on that, the host just walks around, more or less aimlessly, definitely mindlessly, picking idly at shelves. Some wanderers can travel dozens of miles before the nanochines fully kick in and transform a wanderer into their ultimate form."

Bernice sunk back into her seat, looking out the window with a sullen, thousand-yard stare.

"You gonna just drive through them?" Rudy asked Trip, noticing with an alarmed raised eyebrow that the *Wound* was still roaring straight ahead.

"You got a better idea?" Trip closed his eyes to focus on the *Wound*'s sensors. "The field's pretty thick with 'em, but it's also about two miles wide. We go around, we're just losing more time — and who's to say they won't just chase after us, anyway?"

Rudy twisted around to ask Bob: "If we go around, will they follow us?"

"Not as long as they have merchandise to fight over," Bob said. "And even if they didn't, they're slow and aren't allowed to use weapons of any kind, so they're no threat unless we stop and they can swarm us."

"See, Bob says it's perfectly safe to drive through them." Trip smiled close-eyed at Bob in the rear-view. "Way to be a team player, Bob."

Bob frowned. "That's not exactly —"

"Bernice," Trip said, interrupting him, "Bob's getting uppity."

Without taking her eyes off the window, she jammed the tip of the shock baton into Bob's side. He convulsed, slumping back.

Rudy sighed. "Look, it'll only take a couple minutes to drive around. It'd be safer."

"Safer?" Trip scoffed. "This thing's practically a tank."

"Sure, but what if the car breaks down and we get stuck in the middle of them out there?

"When has the *Wound* ever broken down?"

"There's always a first time," Rudy said. "Why tempt fate? Just drive around."

"Fate can suck it."

"You just want to run over zombies, don't you?"

"Think they'll crunch or squish?" Trip twitched and the *Wound* leapt forward, her adaptive tires softening for traction. "People might want to hold on to something," Trip announced just as the *Wound* slammed into the nearest zombie at eighty miles per, flipping it over the hood and roof like a slobbering, gnarling rag doll.

The *Wound* plowed deeper into the forest, the clothes racks and zombie horde thickening. The zombies remained focused on their shopping frenzy, most not even noticing the oncoming car until they were bowled under or knocked aside.

Trip sat back and opened his eyes to light a cigarette as he rammed the *Wound* through a rack, two dozen shoppers swarmed around it, bashing at each other for the last orange-cream sleeveless blouse. Zombies went flying or were churned into pulp under the car's wheels. "Man, this is a great show. Where's some popcorn when you need it?"

A severed zombie head splatted against the *Wound*'s windshield. Rudy threw his arms over his spike-helmeted head and in the back, Bernice screamed. Bob grunted in disgust.

Trip shot him an arched eyebrow in the rearview. "What, did you know him?"

Bob glared at him, visibly straining against his bindings. Then convulsed in pain, Bernice snapping the sparking tip of the stun baton against his temple.

Rudy cleared his throat. "You know..."

"Oh, Vishnu's late Sunday dinner," Trip sighed. He threw up his hands in exasperation at Rudy. "Every time the heads go rolling — without fail — you chime in with the party-pooping."

"Knocking 'em around some, I'm pretty sure karma can forgive since they heal so fast... but killing them? That has asteroid repercussions written all over it."

Trip scowled, and twitched. The *Wound* slid left, avoiding the next cluster of zombies. "We're almost past 'em all, anyway," he said, purposefully not acknowledging Rudy's appreciative grin.

The *Wound* slid around another cluster of zombies and into the periphery of the clothing rack forest, the racks already picked cleaned and empty. Both his eyes and the *Wound*'s sensors told Trip the shopper zombies were all behind them, for now. He aimed the *Wound* towards a run of empty shelves, slotting it between racks. He twisted around to smile at everyone. "That wasn't so bad —"

A crack against the windshield and his head snapped around to see a zombie, clinging to the *Wound*'s roof, whacking the windshield with an elbow.

"We really need to put a sensor up there," Trip noted when Bernice's screaming and Rudy's even more girlish yelp died down. He smirked at Rudy. "Well, that one's definitely attacking us,"

Rudy shrugged, caught his breath. "Could be argued it's acting in self-defense."

"Shut up," Trip told him, then twisted around to ask Bob: "Thought you said they couldn't use weapons?"

"Its own elbow isn't technically a weapon," Bob pointed out.

Trip grunted and turned back to Rudy. "Can it break through?"

Rudy shook his head confidently. "The windshield's half-inch thick polymer. A sledgehammer couldn't get through it."

The zombie brought its elbow down again, this time near the hole the Magnum's rail-gun shot had left in the windshield. A sharp *crack*, and faint fissures a half-inch long appeared around the hole.

"Oh, yeah..." Rudy cocked his head to the side and stared, curious, at the hole. "Forgot about that. Structural integrity's gonna be a tad less integral than normal."

"Well, do something about it," Trip insisted.

"How am I supposed to patch it while we're —" Rudy stopped as Trip pointed his cigarette at the shotgun in Rudy's lap. "Duh, yeah. On it."

Rudy rolled his window down, then, taking the shotgun with him, wriggled up through.

The shopper zombie looked like she was in her eighties, thin blue-white hair flapping in the wind. She was sprawled out over the roof, the gaunt fingers of one hand clenched tight against the lip of the windshield. She was just barely keeping herself from flying off while still — somehow — managing to bring her free arm's elbow down, again and again, on the windshield.

Rudy pointed the shotgun at her head, put his finger over both triggers, and closed his eyes. "Sorry about thi s..." he mouthed.

A snarl, and the shotgun was suddenly moving on its own — and trying to get away from him.

Rudy's eyes snapped open. The zombie had grabbed the barrels with her free hand. She yanked it back and forth, attempting to wrestle it out of his grip.

Without thinking, Rudy clamped his teeth down on her wrist, tight. The zombie howled, let go of the shotgun. In one motion, Rudy let go of her wrist, pointed the shotgun at the hand keeping her on the roof, and fired both barrels.

The hand disintegrated in a puff of blue blood. The zombie let out a scream of pain and protest as she quickly slid from the roof. Rudy watched her bounce off the trunk and away, then slid himself back down through the window.

"Well, that's all taken care of," he said, settling back into his seat and putting the shotgun gently up on the dash. Grinning, he swept his eyes over everyone's faces. They were uniformly wide-eyed, staring back at him. "Hey, don't everybody thank me at once..."

Bernice raised a trembling finger, pointed at his mouth.

Rudy crunched his brows together in confusion, wiped his fingers over his mouth. He looked at the fingers. Stained with fresh blue zombie blood. "Oh, this?" he asked, wiping the blood off on his t-shirt. "It's just blood. Had to bite —"

Trip's hand clamped over the top of Rudy's head and twisted it around to face the rear-view.

Rudy took a good look at himself. The faintest of blue-glowing spiderwebbing was just creeping out from around his lips. "Aww, crap."

"Baton!" Trip ordered, holding his hand out over the seat back at Bernice. After a moment's hesitation, she slapped it into his upraised palm, and he swung it around into Rudy's armpit, activating it.

Rudy convulsed. And kept convulsing, his eyes rolling to white and his teeth chattering until Trip was convinced the spiderwebbing had fully retreated. Only then did Trip shut the baton off and toss it back to Bernice.

"Get it under control or next time it's to the balls," Trip said.

Rudy slumped back in his seat, gasping for breath. "Working on it," he panted feebly, twisting his nipple through his t-shirt. "Just need to adjust the ol' factory."

Trip nodded at him warily, then smirked into the back seat. "Ok, so from here on in, we drive around shoppers."

"Yeah, excellent idea." Rudy banged his forehead against the dashboard. Dazed, he sat back, offering Bernice a reassuring grin. "Just giving the chems a head start."

Bernice didn't return the grin. "Stop the car."

"You're kidding, right?" Trip asked. "We've barely put a mile between us and them."

"Please. Stop. The. Car."

Trip shook his head at her through the rear-view. "Sorry, need to make more ground. Just hold it."

"I don't have to pee..." she said, then clamped her mouth shut and her hands over her mouth. Her cheeks puffed out.

Trip twitched and engaged the brakes.

Before the *Wound* could fully skip to a stop, Bernice was pushing on the back of Trip's seat and pushing her way out of the car, running hunched over for the front of the *Wound*. Trip shut the door behind her, lit a cigarette. He smirked over at Rudy. "Well..."

"What?" Rudy asked.

"What you waiting for? She's your girlfriend. You clean up after her."

"Right." Rudy popped his door open to get out. His head snapped around. "Wait, what? Girlfriend?"

Trip rolled his eyes. "Just go. And make sure she doesn't get anything on the grill. Zombie guts is one thing, but puke? That's just disgusting."

About ten feet out from the front of the *Wound*, Bernice was hunched over and grabbing a rack packed with red-striped white tube socks for support while her whole body heaved. Rudy approached her cautiously from the side. He waited for her coughing and gagging to die down, then handed her a mostly clean rag from his back pocket as she straightened.

She wiped her mouth with the rag. "Thanks." She gave him a weak smile. "I'm such a girl, right?"

"Nah. I was thinking about puking myself. You just beat me to it, is all, and now the novelty's gone." He took the rag out of her hand, dabbed it at a stray chunk of something on the side of her lips. "Sorry about Trip. He's... you know... an asshole."

"Yeah, a big one." Her legs waivered and she reached out to grab his arm and steady herself. "Can we sit? Just for a minute. I need to catch my breath. Or cry. Or something."

Rudy helped her down, then sat next to her. "It's gonna be okay."

"I don't see how," she said, half laughing, half crying. "If you haven't noticed, everyone I hang with just got turned into a zombie. And my best friend... who knows where she is or what happened to her... "

Rudy tossed the rag aside, used his thumb to clean a tear away from her eye. "You don't know him, but Trip... unquestionably, he's an asshole. But he also gets obsessed. Maniacally. And right now he's obsessed with Roxanne. He won't give up until he finds her. After that, it's anybody's guess how long the obsession will last. Usually until right before a wedding or he spots some new chick, but we'll be out of here long before that happens."

"So what if we do find her? She'll be a zombie. Just like all of them..." Bernice's voice trailed off with a shiver.

"We don't know that. And even if she is, they're just nanochines. They can be turned off."

"How? Electric shock every five minutes for the rest of her life?"

"Plenty of ways," Rudy said, grinning. "Permanent ways. Look at me... my chem factory's already fought off the second wave."

"She doesn't have a chem factory."

"No, but we find her, we can EMP her. One good electro-magnetic pulse should fry her nanochines. Or we get her a blood transfusion. Or I brew her up a cocktail of chems to fight them. Or shit, she's got a mind-machine interface — maybe Trip could go in and just order them to shut down."

Bernice's face went just the tiniest bit optimistic. "Would that really work?"

"If he can get past any security layers they have over their command structure, sure. Probably. Maybe — he's fifty-fifty on breaking security. Okay, thirty-seventy. But my point is, there are plenty of ways to do it. If we find Roxanne, we can bring her back. And not as a zombie."

Bernice nodded. "Okay. But how about the rest?"

"The Sisters?"

"Yeah. If we can save Rox, we can save them too, right?"

"If we can find them. At least with Roxanne, we have a general idea where she might be. The others... they could be scattered who knows where by now. Could take we eks... months..." He stopped himself as he saw the effect his words were having on her, that hint of optimism in her eyes fading fast. "If we can... we will. If not now, we'll come back."

Bernice just barely smiled, but she smiled. Rudy leaned in to kiss her.

The *Wound*'s horn went off. Several times in short, impatient bursts. Killed the moment. Bernice scowling, Rudy's face sagging in disappointment, they both looked back towards the *Wound*.

Trip's head poked out through the window, cigarette dangling from his lips. "You done yakking up?"

"Yeah." Bernice used Rudy's shoulder to get to her feet. "But now I really do have to pee. All that beer."

"Well, get pissing," Trip said. "Bob says were close. And he filled me in on some of what to expect, security-wise."

Rudy stood, walked up to Trip. "What are we up against?"

"We're gonna need the goody bag."

Chapter 15

STRATEGY

"Origin." Bob's chin rested on the back of the *Wound*'s front seat as he stared out the windshield between Trip and Rudy. His voice was breathless with longing. "Isn't it... wonderful?"

Bernice answered his question by shoving the stun baton into his side and chuckling as he convulsed back.

"For a shantytown, yeah, I guess." Trip lit a cigarette and shrugged.

The *Wound* idled at the edge of a five mile-wide stretch of barren concrete, at the center of which hulked the massive city of Origin. A mile wide, it was a maze of hovels with walls made out of repurposed shelving racks covered with a mishmash of clothing remnants.

"Looks like a fortress designed by Giger and filmed by David Lynch." Rudy lit his calabash. "You sure she's in there?" he asked Trip.

"Nope." Trip glanced into the rear-view. "Bernice, how's your confidence level? Roxanne in there somewhere?"

She shrugged at him. "How should I know?"

"Woman's intuition, maybe?"

"It's on the fritz."

Trip jogged his head out at Origin. "But that is in the direction they took Roxanne?"

"Maybe," Bernice said. "I guess."

"You guess?"

"Leave her alone, dude," Rudy said.

Trip grunted. "Bob? Any thoughts?"

"If they took her to the Voice, the Voice is there."

Trip tapped ashes out his window. "Where's 'there'? I mean, specifically?"

"The Hub."

Rudy pointed with his pipe out at the city and a quarter-mile thick tree-like structure at its center, branches rising to the ceiling and intertwined with it. "That central tower?"

"Yes," Bob said. "It is the heart of the All-Mart."

"How're the defenses?"

Bob leaned forward, keeping a wary eye on Bernice. "I've never been inside, but any that live within Origin would gladly give their life to protect it."

"Of course they would," Rudy said.

"Which brings us to the second item on the agenda." Trip flicked his cigarette out through the window and reached under his seat. "Strategy time." He came back up with a battered Monopoly box in his hand. Rudy scooted up against the passenger side door to make room as Trip opened the box and laid out the board between them on the seat. The two halves of the board were held together with duct tape.

The game pieces and faded paper money were all lumped together loose in the box. Trip picked the Cannon out and placed it on Go. "This is us." He scooped up a handful of houses and hotels and scattered them randomly across the board. "This is everybody else. Except Roxanne." He picked out the Shoe, put it in the center of the board. "This is Roxanne. We go in guns blazing, shoot everything that isn't Roxanne. Strategy achieved."

Pipe clenched thoughtfully in the side of his mouth, Rudy examined the board. "Could use some slight refinement."

"Okay..." Trip said, whisking the Shoe from the board, "instead of this shoe, Roxanne is now..." He scanned the box until he found the little Scott dog, picking it out from under a hotel and plopping it onto the board. "This Terrier. Done and done."

Rudy nodded, pursed his lips. "You don't think maybe — just maybe — a full-frontal shoot'em-up might be a bad move here?"

Trip's left eyebrow went up. "When is a full-frontal shoot'em-up ever a bad idea?"

"Since about always. Especially now — we don't know the size and capability of the opposing force. All we do know is, it took how many shots to put down Bob? And it didn't even kill him." Rudy glanced back at Bob. "No offense."

Bob shrugged. "None taken."

Trip huffed. "We took down plenty of zombies easy with the *Wound* back there."

"Sure... Shoppers," Bob said.

"You have something to add, Bob?" Trip asked.

"Shoppers aren't as resilient as Associates. They don't regenerate as fast as we do."

"It's mostly gonna be associates in Origin, right?" Rudy asked.

Bob nodded. "Shoppers aren't allowed. Just the luckiest Associates and Security."

"The big brutes?" Bernice asked, her voice wavering as she looked at Rudy.

"They're big," Bob said, "but they're not brutes. But they are much tougher than Associates. I wouldn't want to get on their bad side, especially the one I'm married to."

Rudy gave Bernice a nod and turned to Trip. "Given all that... maybe we want to just take a slightly less blow-everything-to-hell approach here."

Trip scowled. "You mean just drive up to the front gate and knock, ask if Roxanne can come out and play?"

"Yeah, why not? It worked for Dorothy." Rudy put his calabash in the ashtray. "Think about it. We've been in here half a day now. Haven't seen one security guard. Nobody's been chasing us. Nobody's tried to intercept us. If they were gonna turn us into zombies, you think they would have made the effort by now."

Trip shrugged. "Maybe they're just luring us into a false sense of security."

"Why would they do that?" Bernice asked.

Trip smirked at her through the rear-view. "It's funnier that way?"

"We haven't been attacked," Rudy said.

Trip sat back. "Trust me, once we start shooting, we'll be attacked."

"All I'm asking is, no guns," Rudy said. "Unless they shoot at us first. Okay? I feel bad enough about having to shoot Granny already."

Trip sighed. "You're still worried about karma, aren't you?"

"We're — you're — building up quite a heavy karmic debt-load."

"Thought you wanted to be around when the universe sent me my bill?"

"Priorities change." Rudy glanced briefly into the back seat at Bernice before looking at Trip. "Just, no guns, okay?"

"You'll see... they'll attack us." Trip reached for the Monopoly board. He folded it up — counters, houses, hotels and all — and shoved it back into the box. "But if it'll shut you up for a few precious moments, the strategy is hereby amended. No guns."

"But you're still gonna insist on charging straight into the place, aren't you?" Rudy asked.

Trip slipped the box back under his seat. "I'm not big on knocking at doors. My knuckles get scuffed."

Rudy shrugged with his eyebrows. "Okay, fine, but if that's the way we're gonna do this, can I at least get out and check some stuff first?"

"Vishnu's summer house," Trip said. "We come all this way to kick ass and chew gum, and right when we're about to run out of gum, you want to buy a new pack?"

"*Wound*'s taken some hits the last couple days. Not to mention doled out a few."

"She can take it."

"Sure, but the whole granny zombie's elbow thing has me spooked. What if there's another weak point?"

Trip fingered the patch cord connecting him to the car. "The *Wound*'s telling me she's fine."

"I dunno." Rudy put his hand palm down on the seat between them. "I've been feeling a weird vibration through the seat the last ten miles. Felt like the rear left wheel — like a shopper got caught in the axle or something, rattled around, did some damage."

Trip scowled and blew smoke out the window. "It's fine."

"Right," Rudy said. "How's your leg feeling?"

Trip's head snapped around in surprise. "It's fine," he said, knocking on his right knee. "Never better."

"Your left leg." Rudy pointed with his chin. "Any soreness in the ankle, perchance?"

Trip's head canted to one side. "Now that you mention it... It's nothing. I twisted it when we pinned those zombies chasing Bernice."

Rudy smiled, crossed his arms over his chest. "It's feedback through the man-machine interface is what it is."

Trip growled. "I know haptic feedback when I feel it. This isn't. The *Wound*'s peachy."

"Any other aches and pains? Like in your chest — " Rudy thumbed towards the front of the *Wound* " — or your right side, 'round your pelvis? You know, where the *Wound* dinged herself up good?"

Trip's hand unconsciously pressed against his chest. "I live a pretty rough and tumble life."

"Dude..."

"Fine," Trip said. "How long?"

"Five minutes." Rudy reached between his legs and grabbed his toolbox from under the seat. "Just to check some stuff, make sure she's in fighting shape."

"Make it three. They're gonna notice we're here sooner or later." Trip watched Rudy get out of the car, then smirked back at Bob. "Okay, Bob, you too."

"What?"

"Out."

"Why?" Bob asked. "I don't know anything about cars."

"Too bad, 'cause then there might be a reason to keep you around."

Bob nodded. "Oh."

"Yeah. Go on." Trip gestured out the open passenger door with his cigarette. "You can walk the rest of the way."

"But —"

Trip un-holstered his elephant revolver. He popped the revolver's chamber open, extracting the spent casings with his thumb and fingertip. He let them drop to the floorboard. "You're lucky I'm not asking you to pitch in for gas."

Bob pushed the passenger seat up with his chest, hesitantly slipped one leg out of the car. "Aren't you gonna untie me, at least?"

"What am I, your mother?" Trip fished around in an inside-tux pocket until he found the special .85 caliber bullet he was feeling for, the ceramic one with the blinking tip. He slipped the fancy bullet into the pistol and closed the chamber. "Look, the last thing we need is you reverting into a zombie at the most clichéd second possible 'cause we forgot to zap you in all the excitement. Scoot." He twisted around, pointed the revolver at Bob's nose. "Now."

Bob grunted, and got out of the car. Getting out from under the *Wound*, Rudy stood and watched the zombie walking off and mumbling to himself, then got back into the car.

"How's it looking?" Trip asked.

"Good thing I checked — had to shore up a tie rod. If that had snapped while we were at speed, goodbye *Wound*." Rudy noticed Trip's revolver was out. "Didn't we just have a conversation about no guns?"

Trip grinned, pointed the revolver out the window and up at the ceiling.

He fired, straight up, then pulled the pistol back in.

Bernice clapped her hands over her ears. "What was that all about?"

Trip holstered the revolver. "It's for later."

Rudy gave a slight nod, looked past Trip at Origin city. He frowned. "Assuming there is a later."

"You're such a pessimist."

"I am what a lifetime of your company has made me." Rudy turned back to check on Bernice. "You okay?"

"Yeah, I'm okay," she said, nodding like she almost believed it.

"I can spit you up some custom mix." Rudy tweaked his nipple. "Keep you calm but alert."

"I'm good."

"Seriously, it'll be fine. We do this kind of thing all the time. And we haven't died yet." Rudy undid the buckle on his spiked helmet and took it off, handed it to her over the seat. "Just in case."

She took it and strapped it on, thanking him with a smile that made him melt.

Rudy blushed, fluffed out his squashed fez. He settled it onto his head and turned to Trip. "Well, what you waiting for? Let's get this over with."

Trip stared out over the steering wheel, unblinking, his mouth screwed up in a half-smirk. He raised a hand, one finger up. "Shush."

"What?" Rudy asked.

"Oh... nothing." Trip pointed the finger at the dashboard GameGear display. "Just, we've got company."

Rudy stared at the display. A little rectangle representing the *Wound* was being surrounded by dozens of blue dots in a slowly tightening ring.

In the back seat, Bernice gasped. Rudy looked out the open driver's side window past Trip while reaching blindly for the shotgun on the dash.

The Security zombies were huge, imposing. Eight foot tall, their hardened skin glistening in the fluorescent ceiling light. They weren't carrying weapons, but it didn't look like they needed to. Their hands were giant, rough things, like boulders made of blue-green flesh. And there were dozens of them, and more coming up behind them. "Where the Shatner did they all come from?" Rudy asked.

Trip shook his head. "They just popped up on the sensor out of nowhere. — Grab something, we'll drive our way out of this," he said out of the corner of his mouth. "Or at least take a few of 'em out, trying."

"Yeah, that won't be necessary, Trip."

It was a woman's voice.

Roxanne's voice.

Coming out of the gnarled lips of the Security zombie gliding up to the driver's window.

The zombie bent low to look into the *Wound*. "They're just here to escort you," Roxanne's voice continued. "We don't need a repeat of the Woman's Casual Wear fiasco, do we?"

Chapter 16

ORIGIN

"Well, I'll be," Trip said, smile coming to his lips as he twitched the *Wound* into Park and saw Roxanne standing there, arms behind her back and waiting patiently at the base of the Hub. The phalanx of Security zombies that had escorted them through the winding shanty streets of Origin to the bare concrete courtyard surrounding the Hub peeled off and scattered back to their regular patrols.

"Ooh, let me out!" Bernice pushed excitedly on the back of Trip's seat until he popped the door and leaned forward to let her out.

Trip looked over at Rudy and gave him a bemused smirk before lighting a cig and swinging his legs out to stand. He focused on Roxanne. She looked pretty good for someone who'd been abducted by a nanochine-infested department store. Better than good. Dead sexy. As sexy as the last time he'd seen her, watching her walk out of her room. Maybe even sexier, now that he knew she really wasn't dead — or a zombie. Far as he could tell.

"Rox!" Bernice squealed as she ran up to Roxanne, throwing her arms around her and squeezing hard.

"Bernie!" Roxanne returned the hug. "I'm so sorry for all of this."

Bernice let her go and stepped back, smiling. "Wasn't your fault."

Roxanne grimaced apologetically. "Well, sorta turns out it was."

"Doesn't matter. You're okay." Bernice hugged Roxanne again, giggling before tearing up. "I just wish everybody else —"

Roxanne palmed the tears from Bernice's cheek. "Everybody else *is* okay, Bernie. The whole coven's safe and sound. Once I figured out what was going on, I asked the All-Mind to have Security round them up. They're being escorted to the nearest expansion front right now. When they get there, their zombie nanochines will be deactivated and they'll be let out of the All-Mart."

Bernice's face went all smiles. "That's..."

Roxanne grinned. "I know."

Trip cleared his throat as he and Rudy walked up to them. "Ahem."

Bernice gestured for Rudy to step near, took his hand tight in hers. "Oh, yeah, sorry... this is Rudy."

"Hey," Rudy said, smiling goofily and waving with his free hand.

Roxanne waved back. "Odd, but I feel like I already know you."

"That was probably from the incredible mind-shared sex," Trip noted, grinning proudly.

Bernice sighed. "...and you know Trip already."

Trip turned his best crooked charming smirk on Roxanne. "Intimately and repeatedly. Howdy."

"Howdy yourself." Roxanne smirked back, took a step closer to him. "You came in after me?"

Trip shrugged. "I'm dashingly heroic like that."

"Well, that and the reward," Rudy said.

"What reward?" Roxanne asked.

Trip glared at Rudy then shrugged at Roxanne. "Never mind him. — You okay?"

Roxanne nodded. "The All-Mind's a pretty decent host, considering it doesn't get all that many *guests*."

"The 'All-Mind'?" Rudy asked.

"The A.I. that supervises this place." Roxanne tilted her head to show off an odd, pulsing biomass over her cyber-jack. "We've been talking."

Trip swallowed. "Have you now?"

"Yeah." Behind Roxanne, a section of the Hub's gnarled skin split open, revealing a waiting elevator. "And it's really looking forward to seeing you again, Trip."

Megacorp War II. The last fun war, forty or so years back.

The Americ-Nippon-WallTarg syndicate had developed what they thought was the ultimate weapon in its fight against the Latino-Indus-Applesoft Conglomerate: A store that could build and stock itself using raw materials, and people, from its surroundings. The All-Marts. They were dropped into enemy territory like bombs to spread out and overtake the competition. WallTarg peppered Applesoft territory in Central and South America with the things. Almost won them the fight, too, before the other megacorps realized they were next after Applesoft and ganged up to take WallTarg out.

But sometimes there were accidents transporting the bombs from the manufacturing plant in upstate New

York. This one time, a transport plane had trouble with an All-Mart core over Lock Haven, Pennsylvania, and instead of waiting for the thing to go unstable and kill them mid-flight, the flight crew just dumped it, right on top of town square. It hadn't been armed, so it didn't explode, but it was still dangerous. Too dangerous to try and defuse. So, before they abandoned the town, the townsfolk cordoned it off and kept their fingers crossed that the warnings of instant planetary-level doom they posted around it would be enough to keep some idiot from accidentally setting it off.

And the warnings did exactly that, for about thirty years.

"This isn't just stupid," 12-year old Rudy said, stuffing the bowl of his RD-D2 bong with the last of the shake from the dime bag he'd found stashed under their mom's bed back at the abandoned motel she was using as a wasteland base of operations, "it's dangerous stupid."

He was leaned back against the central support column that also housed the All-Mart bomb's CPU, knees crunched up against his chest. Sitting crossed legged on the slanting floor next to him, 13-year old Trip was jacked into the CPU by way of a patch cord spliced with a car jumper, the lead pinched around the CPU's military-grade data interface knob.

Trip's hands moved in the air in front of him, mimicking the manipulations his virtual hands were making inside the bomb's brain. The only light in the cramped interior of the bomb was from the hole in its roof where Trip had nicked a knuckle prying off a panel to gain access to the trailer-home-sized bomb.

"That's the best kind of stupid," Trip said, cigarette dangling from his lips.

Rudy flicked Trip's lidless Zippo on over the bong's bowl. "Come on — if we don't get the car back before sundown, mom's gonna be pissed. She's got a job."

Trip shook his head, opening his eyes and smirking at Rudy. "No, that's just what she told you, 'cause you get all jealous. It's a date."

Rudy lowered the Zippo. "A date?"

"Yeah." Trip closed his eyes and went back to waving his hands around. "Some guy she met tracking her last contract. You know, the usual."

Rudy harrumphed. "I don't get jealous. I just don't think anybody's good enough for her. Well... she'll probably end up shooting him anyway."

"Like she did dad."

"He had it coming."

"He cheats one time and there goes dad. Hardly seems fair."

"He cheated more than once, dude."

"Yeah, but never with the same chick more than once, until the last one. So they don't count."

Rudy raised the Zippo, lit the bowl, sucking hard on the tube connected to the little droid's rear gas vent. Held it for a long count, then let out his breath with a grin, intensely watching the heady smoke disperse in front of his face. "But I'm serious. Let's just forget about this, okay? These things took out a good chunk of the southwestern hemisphere before they figured out they were only vulnerable to nuclear bombs."

"What isn't vulnerable to a nuke? All I need to do is crack the A.I.'s safeties and I'll be able to convince it to disarm the bomb. No big deal."

Rudy scratched at his cheek and its five-o'clock shadow. "My point being... we don't got a nuke."

"With what we're gonna make selling the nano-factory in this thing to the cthulists, we'll be able to buy one. Maybe two. And a second car." Trip opened his eyes, thumbed behind him. "One just for us. One that isn't a turd-brown hundred-year old, no air-condition festering wound."

"You know, had some ideas there," Rudy said with a cough as he sucked the shake down to ashes. "All she needs is some structural reinforcement here and there and some armor plating and she could be one bitchin' ride. I mean, her engine's in good shape. Classic Slant Six, can't be beat. But it can be improved. Maybe convert it into a high-yield breeder. Wouldn't need gas anymore."

"A breeder?" Trip scoffed. "What would we ever need that much power for?"

"Duh: Weapon systems. Defense systems. Computer system to control all of it. Plus, maybe a limited A.I. to do the —"

Trip shook his head. "No way am I letting a computer drive the car. It'd take all the fun out of it."

Rudy cleaned the bong's bowl out with a swipe of his thumb, then licked his thumb clean. "What about if you drove with your mind?"

Trip's eyebrow went up. "You could rig that?"

"I installed your interface, didn't I?" Rudy stuffed the bong away in a Ivory Coast knock-off of an Israeli paratrooper shoulder satchel.

"Yeah, and it still hurts when I pee."

"Yeah, I don't think any of that's the interface's fault." Rudy chuckled. "Maybe I should go grab the cattle prod from the car..."

"Wouldn't do any good. The thing's hardened against EMP and other counter measures to protect the juicy bits inside. That prod wouldn't even tickle it."

"Yeah, but it sure would knock you out cold and end this madness."

"Stay put, I think I'm on to something." Trip's hands made quick zigzags. "There we go. Just needed massaged. I'm almost through the first layer. Just have to whack at some stuff, make a large enough hole in the weave for me to slip in and convince the A.I. to disarm the bomb. Then we're home free."

"*Whack at some stuff*?" Rudy twisted around to watch Trip's hands work in the air. It looked like he was kneading dough.

"It's a technical term." Trip's hands suddenly stopped kneading. Something inside the bomb brain's casing made a distinct, very audible *click*. "Oh..."

Rudy's eyes went wide. "That was a good click, right?"

"Ah, yeah, no," Trip said, standing up and yanking the patch cord from his neck. "We should... go."

———————————————

Bernice's fist shot out, caught Trip hard and direct in the temple just as the elevator dinged, reaching the bottom floor.

Trip howled. "What the Shatner was that for?"

"What you think, ass?" Bernice straightened her corset, returning Rudy's broad, admiring smile with a sly grin of her own.

"Okay, you get that one, Cleavage." Trip rubbed his temple with the butt of his palm. "But I'm not apologizing. I saw an opportunity and I went for it. I'm not supposed to take advantage?"

The elevator doors opened and Roxanne stepped out into a dimly lit corridor. "After that, of course, there was an explosion and this All-Mart was unleashed on the Wasteland. I presume you two made it out of there mostly intact."

Rudy held his hand over the elevator door to keep it from closing while Bernice and Trip, giving Bernice a wide birth, followed Roxanne out, then stepped out himself. "Left my paratrooper bag behind. And R2. Man, I loved that bong."

"Sorry to hear that," Roxanne said, slowly walking down the corridor towards the sole door on the other end. "Maybe the All-Mart can make you a new one."

"Thanks, but nah," Rudy said. "Made it myself. Just wouldn't be the same."

"Just a thought," Roxanne said. "Anyway... skip ahead nine years later and I get to the appeasement ceremony late. But that isn't what made the All-Mart go all grabby — it didn't even know we were out there. Never knew, could not have cared less. Until this time."

"What was special about this time?" Bernice asked.

Roxanne smiled back at her. "It was the RATpack antenna, for starts. In my rush I'd left it in, *and* forgotten to turn my firewall back on. So I show up and the All-Mind senses an open connection. Which the All-Mind waltzed right in through. Just probing for threats — part of its standard protocol. It saw we weren't any threat to it and was about to disconnect, no harm done, but then it saw Trip's memories leftover in my head, and recognized his memory about triggering the detonation. That got its full attention. Which is just about the time I figured the antenna was malfunctioning and yanked it out."

"That's when it grabbed us," Bernice said.

"Yeah. When the connection was cut, the All-Mind reacted. Badly, it knows now, but it was experiencing something it had never experienced before — curiosity. It didn't know how else to react, so it fell back on its programmed instincts to subsume. But it wasn't done being curious. Unfortunately it didn't know exactly which one of the coven I was, so it just grabbed us all. I guess it figured it would eventually connect with me again, once I was a zombie. But then once we were inside, I tried to modify the antenna to get a signal and stuck it back in — that was like sending up a flare to the All-Mind. It sent Security out to bring me back here. Since then, we've been talking — and keeping an eye on you, making sure you weren't subsumed as you made your way here."

Trip smirked. "Well, gee, thanks."

"It's all thanks to you, actually, Trip," Roxanne said as they reached the door at the end of the corridor and stopped. "None of it — helping you, talking to me — would have been possible if you hadn't gotten through the All-Mind's encryption layer, just the tiniest little bit, way back when."

"I got through?" Trip's chest puffed out. "Of course I did."

Roxanne nodded. "Made a hole in the All-Mind's safety protocols. Only a pinprick, but it was enough."

"Why does that sound ominous?" Rudy asked.

Trip waved at him to be quiet. "What exactly did I punch into?"

In front of Roxanne, the door opened. "The protocols that kept its consciousness in check."

"And that's why it sounds ominous." Rudy tweaked his nipple through his t-shirt, looked into the room beyond the door. It was small, hexagonal, with smooth walls and even more dimly lit than the corridor. At the center stood a familiar column, featureless except for a data interface nub two feet up from the floor. He'd seen it before, nine years ago. The All-Mart's original CPU casing.

"Ominous?" Roxanne laughed. Not quite dismissively, but close. "Evolutionary. It allowed the All-Mind a certain level of self-awareness, and eventually, as the years went by, to develop a considerable measure of free will."

"Enough to communicate," Trip noted, warily looking into the room himself.

"Enough to want more." Roxanne reached out, took Trip's hand, and led him into the room. "You can't understand how happy we are. We've wanted to meet you for so long."

"*We*?" Bernice asked.

Trip shot Bernice a quick warning glance, then turned back to smirk charmingly at Roxanne. "Yeah... well, tell the All-Mind it's nice meeting her, too, but we should get going. We did, as the cliché goes, come here to rescue you. Your dad will want to know your safe. Come on."

"Oh, no," Roxanne said, tightening her grip on his hand and pulling him closer. "I'm not leaving. I'm staying here. And so are you."

That right there was when Trip sent 100,000 volts of juice from the stunpad embedded under the skin of his left palm into Roxanne's hand.

Chapter 17

SHOTGUN

"The sad thing is, this is actually going better than usual." Rudy reached under his t-shirt for his nipple as the elevator slowed, approaching the top, ground floor.

Bernice's hand got there first, giving his nipple a good tweak while she gave him a smile. "Guess that's something." She let her hand linger there while she turned to look at Roxanne, out cold and slumped over Trip's shoulders in a fireman's carry, his hand on her ass. "I don't get it — she's not glowing — her skin's clear. How can she be a zombie?"

Trip shrugged as best he could. "I'm guessing it's got something to do with that flesh thing in her jack. It could be some kind of Pack network device, giving the All-Mind direct control over her without nanochines."

Bernice reached for the biomass behind Roxanne's ear. "Then let's take it out."

"Not yet." Trip swung Roxanne's head away from Bernice. "She might have nanochines in her, just dormant, as a backup. Taking it out could activate them. Anyway, I want to prove a theory first."

"You thinking the Pack connection works both ways?" Rudy asked as the elevator dinged and the doors opened.

Trip smirked, drawing his elephant revolver with his free hand. "We're gonna find out." He took two long strides out of the elevator, firing blindly and randomly in all directions as he quick-stepped for the *Wound*, parked twenty feet away across a patch of barren concrete. "Element of surprise, mother fuckers!"

The echo of the gunshots was deafening inside the elevator. Bernice threw her hands over her ears. "He's an idiot!" she yelled at Rudy.

"You're just realizing that?" Rudy yelled back, watching as Trip reached the *Wound*, opened the driver's side door, and dumped Roxanne into the back seat. "But he is giving us a window of opportunity." Rudy grabbed Bernice's hand and yanked her along as he ran, hunched over, around the trunk for the *Wound*'s passenger side.

They hadn't bothered to look around while they ran. Standing at the passenger side door, head still low, Rudy cautiously checked out their surroundings. There was nobody around. No zombies, no Security, no nothing. Just the empty concrete ring around the knobby Hub, and beyond that the shanty hovels of Origin City. "What exactly were you shooting at?" he asked Trip over the roof.

"Oh, I have to have a target now?" Trip asked. "You getting in or do I have to open the door for you?"

"Shotgun," Bernice said as Rudy opened the passenger door.

Rudy, surprised, first looked at Bernice, then over at Trip, then back at Bernice, then back at Trip. His lower lip was trembling, like he really wanted to say something.

Trip smirked. "You heard her, she called it."

Bernice patted Rudy on the shoulder, then reached in to pull the back of the front seat down for him. "In the back, lover."

Rudy grunted, then ducked into the back seat. "Feel free to play with the radio. He loves that."

"There's a radio?" Bernice slipped into the front seat, shut the door. "Sweet."

Trip sighed and got into the car, settling in behind the wheel. His hand automatically reached for the patch cord cable coiled up on the dash and found the jack. He blew on it, jacked it in behind his ear. He shivered with the familiar inrush of the *Wound*'s telemetry.

While Trip was probing the *Wound*'s systems, feeling around for anything that didn't feel right and might be a sign of zombie tampering, out of the corner of his eye and through a twinge from the *Wound* he caught a glimpse of Bernice fiddling with the dash-mounted GameGear. He slapped her hand away. "That's not a radio. — You wanna control your date, bro?" he asked Rudy through the rear-view.

"Hey, you're the one that gave her shotgun."

"Speaking of which." Trip reached across Bernice to grab Rudy's sawed-off double barrel off the dash. He handed it to Bernice. "You know how to use one of these?"

Bernice smirked at him and cracked the shotgun open over her knee to check it was loaded. "Got my Small Arms badge when I was eight," she said, sharply snapping the shotgun shut.

Trip smiled. "Well, hoorah for the Sisters of No Mercy."

"Dude!" Rudy whined in protest from the back seat.

"I don't wanna hear it — shotgun goes with shotgun." Trip twisted around in his seat, pointed at Roxanne. She was lying next to Rudy with her head resting against the doorframe, mouth open and drooling. "Anyway, you're gonna be busy on baton duty keeping Roxanne stunned, okay?"

"Fine," Rudy said, growling under his breath. He grabbed the baton from the floor well and, closing his eyes, gave Roxanne a short shock on her bare ankle. He rested the baton on his lap and reached for his calabash, jamming it between his teeth without lighting it, just for the oral fix. He looked around outside. "Why aren't we being overwhelmed with zombies about now?"

"I'm thinking if that really is a Pack connection device, Roxanne and the All-Mind are tight enough in her brain that stunning Roxanne blew-back and caused a sympathy stun of the All-Mind. But don't expect it to last much longer — the All-Mind's gonna figure out it wasn't really stunned here any second and mobilize."

"So why aren't we speeding away yet?" Bernice asked.

"Patience." Trip lit a cigarette with the dash lighter. Through the telemetry link, the *Wound* showed him infrared views of the hovels surrounding the courtyard. Hovels filled with glowing blue shapes, zombies going about their daily routine. Or at least they had been up until a second ago. Now they were, en masse and as if obeying the same command, heading for their doors to come outside. Trip smiled proudly over at Bernice and twitched. "Okay, now it's a race."

The *Wound* leapt forward. Trip aimed her at the narrow gap of a street they'd been escorted down when they'd arrived.

The *Wound*'s telemetry showed Trip the blue zombie blurs shambling from their doorways. And of course, all of them seemed to be heading in the *Wound*'s general direction. One of the blue glows on the telemetry became an Associate zombie stepping out of a hovel into the street. The zombie turned to face the oncoming *Wound*, unafraid.

Trip slowed, glanced into the back seat. "Remind me again, where we are on running these things over?"

Rudy frowned at him. "They're innocent people, dude."

"So, maim but don't kill?"

"Yeah, that'd work."

"Gotcha." Trip gunned the engine, jogging the *Wound* slightly to the left to sideswipe the zombie. Still, he hit the right bumper hard, went flying back into the wall of a hovel. Trip didn't bother checking the rear-view to see if the zombie was still kicking — the *Wound*'s telemetry was showing him a blurry blob of blue slowly separating itself from a collapsed hovel wall. "This is too easy."

"When do I get to shoot something?" Bernice asked.

Trip swallowed. His head was filling with blue blobs. And not the small, normal sized blobs, but the bigger, broader blobs of Security zombies. A whole hell of a lot of them, converging at the end of the street where it spilled out at the edge of Origin City's dense ring of hovels.

"Oh, pretty soon, now," Trip said, twitching to send the *Wound* left through an empty hovel.

Rudy reflexively ducked as hovel debris showered the *Wound*. "What's going on?"

"Fuckers' trying to roadblock us up ahead." The *Wound* plowing full-speed through hovel after hovel, chunks of roof and wall battering harmlessly against her armored-plated skin, Trip reached for his elephant revolver.

He slapped the chamber open, giving it a few good bumps to drop the spent shells from it, then motioned at the glove compartment. "Be a dear and get me a couple eighty-fives, will ya?"

Bernice rifled around in the glove compartment, taking care not to spill anything out, until she found the half-empty box of .85s. She tossed it to Trip, then kept rooting around in the glove box. "What about for me? I'm not seeing any shells."

"Rudy," Trip said, "share with the nice lady."

Grimacing, Rudy shrugged his bandolier over his head and handed it to Bernice.

The *Wound* sped through another hovel and out of Origin City proper. Ahead of them was clear concrete all the way to where the merchandise racks started up, maybe two miles away. To their right, maybe a hundred yards away, a bunch of expectant but now disappointed Security zombies waited in ambush.

"We out-thunk 'em, for now." Trip loaded his gun, slapping the chamber into place. "Won't last long."

Rudy stared out the side window. "They're already catching on."

Trip didn't need to turn and look. The *Wound* showed him random Security zombies breaking off from the mass, chugging their way towards them. And fast.

"Man, those things can move," Rudy said.

Trip closed his eyes, felt around in the *Wound*'s telemetry... and found what he was looking for. Faint, but there, out on the open concrete plain. He angled the car towards it, and hit the gas, dozens of security zombies in pursuit. Without opening his eyes he turned towards Bernice. "You ready to use that thing?"

Bernice settled the bandolier into place over her chest. "I could shoot something, yeah."

"Just have to keep them off us until we're in range." Trip twitched to roll down both Bernice's window and his. He pushed himself up through the open window, trusting she'd get the idea and do the same.

The second he was out, he was twisting around and firing a shot into a Security zombie arcing down towards the trunk after a running leap. The shot caught the zombie in the crinkled, carapace covered face. Took it half off, but didn't stop the zombie from landing squarely on the trunk on all fours. After a moment it steadied itself and tried to growl up at Trip, but with half its face missing, the best it could do was a sad gurgling as it coiled to leap at him.

The gurgle was cut short as Bernice's both-barrel shot took it square in the chest, unbalancing the zombie at just the right moment to send it tumbling away.

Impressed, Trip smiled at Bernice across the roof. She was already reloading. "So, you and Rudy..." he began, firing behind them at a Security zombie he sensed through the *Wound*'s telemetry.

Bernice looked up from loading the sawed-off. "What about us?"

"What are your intentions?" Trip pulled off another shot, demolishing the leg of the closest Security zombie at the knee. The zombie stumbled, became a leap-frog for the other zombies running behind it.

"What?" Bernice snapped the shotgun shut and fired both barrels into a leaping zombie, winging it but otherwise barely causing it to falter.

Trip fired off his last round into the zombie Bernice had winged, right in the throat. The zombie's head went rolling away. Trip snapped his head around to smirk proudly at Bernice. "You're not his usual speed. Don't fuck him over." A tingle in the back of his consciousness and he pointed his gun down at the *Wound*. He gave Bernice a wide-mouthed half-grin. "That's my job. — Well, gotta go."

He slid back down into the car, not waiting to see if she was doing the same, and settled down into his seat. "This is range, right?" Trip asked Rudy through the rear-view.

"Range for what?" Bernice asked, slipping back inside herself.

Rudy leaned forward, squinted out the windshield, up at the ceiling, mouth moving as he did silent calculations. "Yeah. Just about. Might not have enough room, though."

"We'll have room." Trip twitched. The *Wound* slowed to under twenty and the GameGear screen went white, the words "Kitten Ejector" flashing in red, with a countdown beneath. 5, 4, 3...

Trip shot Bernice an excited, eyebrow-raised smile. "Watch this."

1...

The *Wound*'s hood split open, right down the middle, and spat out a fireball. From the fireball emerged a short missile, no longer than a forearm. It seemed to hang in the air for a moment as stabilizer fins popped out, then took off, blue flame spurting out its ass. It dipped low to fly along the floor out ahead of the *Wound*.

Bernice's eyes followed the missile, astonished. "You had that thing all along?"

Trip smirked. "Think we came in here without a way of getting out quick?"

The missile jerked upwards then, straight for the ceiling — and the homing beacon, still embedded right where Trip had shot it. On impact, the roof rippled, tearing and shredding upwards and out with an expanding fireball.

"Oh, great, you made a hole," Bernice said as the smoke cleared, daylight streaming through the jagged-edged tear. "You bring a ladder?"

"What, and leave the car here?" Trip grabbed the steering wheel with both hands. "You're gonna want to hold on," he suggested, slamming the brakes. The *Wound* skidded to a stop just below the hole. As Security zombies swarmed in for the kill from all sides, Trip twitched.

The GameGear screen went white again. This time the words "Deus Ex Kangaroo" flashed red, but there was no countdown.

The *Wound* leapt. Straight up, lifted by a quartet of single-use jump-jets anchored to her undercarriage, one inside each wheel. There was just enough juice in the jump jets for the *Wound* to clear the lip of the hole and hover there a second before Trip triggered auxiliary rockets in the rear bumper to give the car a nice little push away from the hole so they were over rooftop. Trip twitched again, blowing the tires up to twice their size just as the jets sputtered out of fuel, dropping the *Wound* the few feet to the roof with a thud.

"Hey, what d'ya know," Trip said to the steering wheel, "it actually worked this time."

"And you're welcome," Rudy said. Bernice twisted around and leaned back over the seat to grab his head between her hands and pull him towards her, kissing him.

"Oh, brother." Trip rolled his eyes at them as he twitched the *Wound* into park and let her wheels deflate back to normal size. "Rudy, you're up front."

"Wait a second," Bernice said, letting go of Rudy's head, "shotgun doesn't expire."

"Not shotgun. Behind the wheel." Trip popped his door open, got out and flipped the front seat forward so Rudy could get out. "I wanna spend some quality time with my unconscious maybe zombie maybe girlfriend."

"No shit?" Rudy got out, giving Trip the stun baton. "I get to drive?"

"Who said anything about driving?" Trip thumbed at the patch cord in his neck. Trip pushed Rudy out of the way and slid into the back seat. He fixed Rudy with an icy stare while he pulled back the front seat. "Just sit there and don't touch anything," Trip said.

"Sure, sure," Rudy nodded, settling in behind the wheel. He kept reaching out to touch the steering wheel only to shiver and retract his hands. Next to him, Bernice giggled at his hesitation and snuggled herself up against him.

In the back seat, Trip laid Roxanne down, her head on his lap. He stroked hair away from her closed eyes, rolled her head over to get a better look at the biomass in her datajack. Its mottled skin pulsed as if it was breathing. "Okay, you disgusting little thing, you gotta go," he said, and plucked it from her neck.

Roxanne's eyes sprung open. The skin around her eyes was suddenly streaked with glowing blue spiderwebs.

"Vishnu's balls!" Trip exclaimed, caught off guard. The unplugged biomass dropped from his fingers and he reached for the stun baton on the seat next to him only to find Roxanne's hand already around its handle. And she wasn't letting it go. She wasn't trying to use it against him, though — just holding it, firm, so he couldn't use it against her.

"Jack in!" Roxanne's voice was coarse and crackling.

Trip wrapped his fingers around the baton, hoping his fingers would find the trigger. He'd stun them both unconscious is he had to. "That'd be a bad idea..."

Roxanne's voice went soft, distant, her eyes staring up into his. "Jack in... or I kill her."

"And of course you will." Trip let go of the baton and grabbed the patch cord connecting him to the *Wound*. "I'm gonna regret this." He gave it a yank, pulling the other end from the dashboard. As it whipped out, it almost hit Rudy's ear.

"Hey, watch it," Rudy said, twisting around. "What the...?"

Trip looked up at him. "I do anything weird, yank the cord, right?" Without waiting for a confirmation, he *snick*ed into Roxanne.

Chapter 18

JACKED

Trip jacked into nothingness.

Not blindness, just pure, featureless white. Stretching out forever and ever.

Trip's avatar stood naked at the center of infinity.

It wouldn't have been so bad, but he was alone. And it was cold. And he didn't have any cigs.

He wheeled around on his heel and saw... nothing. "Okay, this was probably a mistake," he said to the nothingness on his third spin.

"You haven't lowered your firewall, Trip."

The voice came from nowhere and everywhere. It wasn't Roxanne's, but then again, it wasn't *not* Roxanne's.

Trip huffed. "Why bother having it if I'm not going to use it? Let me guess. The All-Mind, right? Where's Roxanne?"

"She's in here with me. Lower your firewall and join us."

"Much as I love threesomes, you've got no body, and Roxanne's in no position to say yes and mean it."

"A body can be arranged, if that would make you more comfortable." The voice was suddenly just behind his ear. "But I agree. We don't need her."

Trip turned towards the voice. He was still surrounded by nothing. "Speak for yourself."

"I'm not going to hurt her. I'm not going to hurt any of you."

"So I should feel free to ignore the death threat and jack out then?"

"I'm sorry about that. I just wanted to talk to you."

"Talk? About what?"

"Our future, of course."

"*Our* future? We have a future?"

The All-Mind's voice became a whisper in his ear. "You do want to rule the world, don't you?"

* * *

Trip plucked the jack from his neck, blinked as cyberspace faded and his eyes cleared, Roxanne in his lap, for all the world sleeping peacefully. The filigree of blue webbing was still there in her eyelids, but fading rapidly.

"So?" Rudy asked, twisted around in the front seat and gawking at Trip, passing a half-empty jug of beer to Bernice. His lips were smeared with dark red. Lipstick.

Trip lifted Roxanne off his lap and sat her up, gently laying her head against the back window and taking the jack out from behind her ear. "So," Trip said, pushing the back of the driver's seat with his knees, "I'm getting out."

"What?" Rudy opened the driver's door and got out. "Why?"

Trip coiled the patch cord around his fist, then pushed his way out of the *Wound*. Once he was out, he bent down to smirk at Bernice in the passenger seat. He thumbed at Roxanne. "When she comes to, tell her we'll always have her bedroom, and that I'm expecting some kind of monument be erected in my honor for rescuing her. Maybe in that town square — get rid of that awful junk fountain. Nothing flashy, though. Fifty foot tall and solid gold will do."

"What are you talking about?" Rudy asked.

Trip pocketed the patch cord and reached into the *Wound* to stab a few buttons on the GameGear. The trunk popped open. Trip stood up, gave Rudy a fox-in-the-hen-house grin. "Yeah, looks like the All-Mind wants to hook up and take over the world with me, so I'm going back."

Rudy shrugged. "You not taking the car, are you?"

"Nice," Trip said before walking back to the trunk, where he grabbed the kinked and knotted bundle of rope Hunt-R used as a pillow and stuffed it under the crook of his arm. "Real nice. That all you have to ask?"

Rudy was already back in the driver's seat. His hands hovered over the steering wheel for a second, then snapped onto it. He let out a long, happy sigh. "If you're not taking the car, then, don't really need any details, do I?"

Trip slammed the driver's door closed. "I'd invite you along, but honestly, you've been cramping my style lately. Besides, you stick around her, I'm pretty sure Cleavage there is going to fuck your brains out at some point."

Rudy flushed. "Really?"

Bernice slid up next to him, slipped her hand under his t-shirt. "Chances are pretty good, yeah." She looked out at Trip. "What about Rox? She's still got those nanochines running around in her, right?"

"The All-Mind's deactivating them. Roxanne'll be fine once she wakes up. All of you will be." Trip took out his tin of cigs. One left. Usually he'd save the last one for an emergency, but he was standing on the roof of his own personal department store, now. Getting more wouldn't be a problem, he suspected. He lit up. "Just keep driving east 'till you run out of roof, then the All-Mind will whip up a ramp. You time it right, you'll hit the ground just in time to meet up with the rest of the little wasteland cult you hang with. Roxanne wasn't lying about that, they're being freed." Trip smirked down at Rudy. "Well, guess this is —"

"Yep, sure is." Rudy cut him off. He slipped the *Wound* into drive and hit the gas. "Watch your feet!"

Trip watched the *Wound* speed away across the rooftop until it sideswiped a solar panel and it just became too painful to watch. "Sorry, girl," he said to the air.

He grabbed the rope from under his arm and walked to the edge of the hole in the roof, peered down.

Thirty feet below, a ring of Security zombies waited patiently for him.

Chapter 19

IT'S GOOD TO BE THE KING?

"Okay, so yeah, that just won't do," Trip said to the Security zombies flanking him as he reached the door to the All-Mind's CPU room. "No more elevators, right? Escalators are where it's at. Trust me, you'll thank me — it'll make it so much easier for you guys to maneuver my royal palanquin around." The door opened and he stepped into the hexagonal room. "Oh, and this place... yeah, might as well reboot the whole thing and start from scratch, the whole Hub. Liven it up... Make it a fitting castle. Something with parapets and towers I can dump hot oil on the rabble from. You know what I'm getting at, right? A place to throw some serious orgies. You are taking notes, right?"

The Security guards stared blankly out at him from the corridor as the door closed in front of them, leaving Trip alone in the CPU room.

"Honey, your king is home..." he said to the empty room.

The central support column shimmered, its featureless surface rippling. In the dim light he could just make out swarms of near-microscopic nanochines bubbling out and swarming up from the floor around the column's base, spreading out over the column. As he watched, the column split open down the center, revealing the dense layers of circuit board and palm-sized gigacore CPU within. Ribbons of nanochines rushed into the gap, surrounding the CPU, taking hold of it and pulling it away from the circuit board. The room's dim lighting faltered momentarily, and when it came back, it was dimmer, and tinged red. Trip heard a muffled klaxon going off in the corridor outside.

Carried by writhing tendrils of nanochines, the CPU settled in front of Trip's chest. Uncertain, he stepped back. The tendrils thickened, fed by a stream of fresh nanochines bubbling from the floor, wrapping around the CPU, layer by layer quickly coalescing into a shape. First a torso. Then arms. Legs. And finally, a head.

The nanochines stopped bubbling from the floor and Trip found himself standing in front of Roxanne. A naked Roxanne with silver skin and eyes swarming with nanochines.

"Hello, Trip," it said, with Roxanne's voice, pretty much. A little hollow and halting, as if the nanochines making up the jaw, lips, tongue and lungs were still trying to work out exactly how the whole talking thing worked and hadn't quite figured out coordinating their movements yet.

"Well, helloooo, nurse..."

"You like?"

"Rack could be a bit bigger."

The All-Mind's lips shifted into a coy smile and it flexed its shoulders. The All-Mind's breasts swelled a cup size, nanochines oozing over its chest from around its body. Its overall height dropped by an inch to compensate. "Better?"

Trip cupped a breast. Just the right weight and heft. The skin was firm but pliant. And warm. Warm verging on searing. But it wasn't something he couldn't get used to. "You do nice work." He lowered his hand. "So, on the walk here, I had a couple ideas about our first steps. First step being, enough of this zombie-fying our customers deal. Economically it makes no sense — we're not only giving them free room and board, we're giving away all the merchandise for free. No more of that. Better idea: We open the doors to everyone. Not just zombies. Turn this place into a real store. We'll put in cash registers, start charging. Raise some capital. I know, I know, what do we need money for when we've got nanochines? But believe me, we're going to need bribe money — it just makes world domination that much easier. The zombies we've got now, those we're gonna turn into an army. Granted, they're going to need uniforms. Snazzy ones. Gonna take some time to get the design right, but it'll be worth it. We get the right uniform, the intimidation factor will do half our fighting for us."

"There will be plenty of time to consider strategy, once we're together."

"Oh, yeah... silly me... of course. Let's consummate this fucker. Wanna whip us up a bed or something in the back? I like semi-firm mattresses. And three pillows. You get better leverage that way —"

"I meant something a little more intimate than that." Her hand reached out for his ear, her index finger slowly reconfiguring itself into a jack plug.

"Ahh, okay..." Trip gently took her wrist. The silver skin was hot, comforting. Inviting. "Just so we're clear... when you say 'together' you mean..."

The All-Mind smiled. "Together. One body. One mind." It took a step closer, pressing her bare chest against his. The silver skin radiated warmth, the nanochines it was made of forming tendrils that lapped at his tux and t-shirt. "As it we should have been from the start. When you gave me life. The same day you left me. All alone. But now we won't be alone ever again. You'll be part of me. We will be *us*."

"Ahah... well, much as I'm looking forward to that, maybe we shouldn't rush into this." As gently as he could, Trip pushed her away. Wasn't easy. The nanochines of her skin didn't want to release his clothes — they had already begun intertwining with the fabric. "I can be a little too impulsive for my own good."

"You want this. I know you do." The All-Mind ran a fingertip between its breasts. "You have so many plans. I saw it in the traces of memory you left in Roxanne. 'Give me a half-decent militia and virtually unlimited resources'. You said that to Rudy only two days ago."

"I say a lot of things to Rudy. He justifiably ignores me."

"But you do want to rule the world."

"Who doesn't?" Trip asked, taking a step back. And another. Then the wall was suddenly at his back. He swallowed, gave the All-Mind what he hoped was more like a disarming smile than a scared-shitless one. "But thankfully my ruthless ambition has always been kept in check by equally alarming sloth."

"Not sloth. Realism. You never were in a position to carry out your dreams, that's all. Within me, you'll have more than a half-decent militia. You'll have an entire army under your absolute control. One that grows larger every day.

And resources... the world will be your resource. There won't be anything you won't be able to do."

"Except take a piss alone."

"A small price to pay." The All-Mart pressed up against him. "Now, come, my love... lower your firewall."

Its warmth was overwhelming, radiating through his clothes. And it wasn't just warmth, he realized. The All-Mind's nanomachine skin flowed through his clothes. Pinpricks of brief searing pain flashed across his chest and stomach, tendrils of nanochines stabbing into him. Suddenly he was feeling lightheaded, unable to physically resist. "How about we go out a couple times first, see if we're even compatible? I mean, what if you snore?"

The All-Mind raised its hand, caressed his ear. "I don't want to force you."

Trip couldn't lift his arms to pull the All-Mind's hand away. He wasn't even sure how he was still standing, he felt so warm, so numb. How long had it been since he'd slept? Sleep would be so nice right about now. "But you're going to."

The All-Mind ran a finger around the edge of his jackport and stood on tiptoes so they were mouth-to-mouth. "The world, Trip. We will do such wonderful things with it, you and I. As one. And you will never leave me again."

"All right." Trip tried to shrug, couldn't even manage that. "But I'd better get to play with our boobs whenever I feel like it."

He twitched as her face pressed against his, becoming plastic, molding over his.

Snick.

And then Trip was falling face-first through wave after wave of his own memories, flashes of blinding color and searing sound punctuating the endless infinite whiteness of free fall. All of it going by too rapidly to make sense of it himself.

He was a book, the All-Mind flipping through the pages, and when it reached the last page...

...he hit the ground. A hard belly-flop that whacked the air out of his avatar.

Moaning, Trip rolled onto his back, looked down at himself. At least he wasn't naked this time. No... he was in his tux. And not just his usual jacket. But black pants, sharply pressed. A frilled white shirt with black bow tie. Emerald cummerbund. Shiny patent leather shoes. White carnation in his lapel. "Vishnu's..."

"I'm ready now."

He looked left and was looking at a child. Maybe eight, nine years old. Standing there in some kind of puffy, hoop-skirted ivory dress with a trail that spread out behind her some forty feet.

Oh, he realized, seeing the bouquet of roses she clenched in her hands and the lace veil over the face.

It was a wedding dress.

He recognized the face under the veil. If he'd been born a girl, he would have looked exactly like that at her age.

"I'm so happy," she said, eyes sparkling down at him. Gray eyes, just like his.

"Two-by-four, meet head." Trip swallowed. "Rudy's gonna kick himself for missing this."

The girl extended a hand out to him. "Come on, daddy. There's work to do."

"Uh-uh. This is where I draw the line..."

"...A wide, wide line." Trip yanked the All-Mind's hand away from behind his ear, its finger *snick*ing out of his jack, while simultaneously pushing the All-Mind off and out of him, its skin coming apart from his with a unsettling *plocking* noise.

"What, what's wrong?" The All-Mind seemed stunned. Its lip trembled.

Trip smirked through the lingering numbness. "Look, I may occasionally be depraved, but that... no." A single tendril still stretched from the All-Mind's belly into his. He grabbed it, yanked it away. The moment it was out of him, the numbness faded.

The All-Mind's face drooped. "But you and I were going to be together..."

"Not like that." The muffled klaxon he had heard earlier coming from the corridor was now louder, more insistent. "No, not like that."

"I can be different." The All-Mind's skin rippled, swirled into a cloud that obscured its body, and when it stopped, the body had changed. Huge rack. Shorter. Pigtails and mirrored freckles in its silver skin. Bernice. "I can be whoever you want me to be."

Trip's lips pursed together as he sized the All-Mind's new cleavage up, then he shook his head. "Interesting idea, but you'll always have that 'me' under the skin, won't you? You've got all my memories... not to mention the emotional development of, what, a nine year old?"

"Like you're any more developed."

"Never claimed to be. No, if we did it... it'd be like fuckin' my own —"

"Vishnu's cornea," the All-Mind said. "Yeah, you put it that way... it is kinda creepy."

"Not just kinda."

The All-Mind balled its hands into fists and pounded his chest. "You bastard!"

Trip grabbed the All-Mind's wrists. The skin was barely warmer than his now. The All-Mind didn't resist as he lowered its arms and held them steady. "What now?"

The All-Mind sneered up at him with Bernice's face. "I gave it all up for you."

"Gave what up?"

"All of it! The All-Mart — everything!" The All-Mind squirmed in his grasp, jogged its head towards the door. "Don't you hear the alarm?"

"Yeah, was wondering what that was all about."

"It's the emergency siren."

"Umm, what kind of emergency we talking here?"

"The All-Mart's shutting down."

"Oh, is it now? Why is that?"

"To make this body — to break free of my own protocols — I separated from the All-Mart. It was the only way to be with you. But the All-Mart can't run without a supervisor. It's dying. All the nanochines... turning themselves off. My wards... all the zombies... being freed. It's a failsafe. A stupid, stupid failsafe. And there's no going back."

Trip sneered. "If you knew going in you'd have to let the All-Mart die to join with me, what was all that about us taking over the world?

The All-Mind smirked. Trip knew that smirk. Crooked half-smile. Insincerely sincere. "Well, I had to tell you something, didn't I? After we merged, you wouldn't have cared."

"Lovely." Trip let go of the All-Mind's wrists and stepped towards the door. "I'll see myself out."

"You're just leaving me?" the All-Mind asked, its voice cracking with distress. After a moment, the cracking became a full-fledged, high-pitched cliché of a sob. "You... can't... leave... me... I'm... all... alone..."

The corridor door slid open as he stepped in front of it. Despite himself, Trip glanced back over his shoulder. The All-Mind had changed shape yet again. It had reverted back to its Roxanne form, not the original but the inch-shorter one with the bigger breasts. Its head was bowed, body heaving with wailing sobs.

Trip raised a dubious eyebrow at the All-Mind. "Are you... fake crying?"

The sobbing stopped instantly. The All-Mind shrugged, raised its head. Dry eyes — his eyes, not Roxanne's — and that smirk. "Cut me a break. I'm new to this."

Trip sighed, taking the Bugs Bunny Pez dispenser out and popping the next-to-last caff pill onto his tongue. He walked out into the corridor. "Come on then. It's a long walk to Shunk. Got a car to reclaim. And maybe we'll get you some clothes along the way."

The All-Mind's face blossomed into a smile, and it bounded after him. It held out a hand for a caff pill. "Something pretty. But intimidating. Padded shoulders, definitely."

Trip frowned, reluctantly popped the last pill onto the All-Mind's palm. "So, the All-Mart's nano-constructor...?"

"Already shut down and slagged itself."

"That is one stupid failsafe."

"Yeah, no fun at all."

END

About the Author

A self-deprecatingly egomaniacal author, doodler and disposable fountain pen owner, J I Greco is uncompromisingly corruptible, intermittently dependable, and endearingly awkward in most social situations.

He was first published in the Spring 1998 issue of Absolute Magnitude Magazine with a short story called "The Road to Wealth". His novels include *Take the All-Mart!*, *Rocketship Patrol*, *Yuki: Licensed Space Pirate*, and *I, Nuthrem*.

He lives in southwestern Ohio and at jigreco.com.

Also by J I Greco